MAGIA D'AMORE

MAGIA D'AMORE

Murray Pomerance

SUN & MOON PRESS
LOS ANGELES • 1999

Sun & Moon Press
A Program of The Contemporary Arts Educational Project, Inc.
a nonprofit corporation
6026 Wilshire Boulevard, Los Angeles, California 90036
http//:www.sunmoon.com

First published in 1999 by Sun & Moon Press
10 9 8 7 6 5 4 3 2 1
FIRST EDITION
©1999 by Murray Pomerance
Back cover material ©1999 by Sun & Moon Press
All rights reserved

This book was made possible, in part, through contributions to
The Contemporary Arts Educational Project, Inc.,
and a grant from The National Endowment for the Arts

NATIONAL
ENDOWMENT
FOR THE
ARTS

Some of these stories previously appeared in
The Kenyon Review, Descant, and *New Directions in Prose and Poetry 55*

Cover: Joseph Cornell, *A Dressing Room for Gille,* 1939
Mixed media box construction
Richard L. Feigen, New York
Design: Katie Messborn
Typography: Guy Bennett

LIBRARY OF CONGRESS CATALOGING IN PUBLICATION DATA
Pomerance, Murray [1946]
Magia d'Amore
p. cm — (Sun & Moon Classics: 169)
ISBN: 1-55713-308-5
I. Title. II. Series.
811'.54—dc20

Printed in the United States of America on acid-free paper.

CONTENTS

To NM

Objective evidence and certitude are doubtless very fine ideals to play with, but where on this moonlit and dream-visited planet are they found?

—WILLIAM JAMES, 1897

Je veux faire parler les silences de l'histoire.

—MICHELET, 1839

Magia d'Amore

PROFESSEUR PANTALON is beside himself with grief, a fat bird he has brought home for dinner, and for which he has handed over twenty pieces of silver, turning out not to be nearly as dead as promised and walking into the street in an unguarded moment. His estimable wife, Madame Leda, whose bosom is always weighty with considerations, is beside herself with consternation, a silver candelabrum with four cherubim having disappeared from her serving board where it had been standing next to the platter all polished for the stuffed goose. She frames her lips into the shape of a heart and flies through the house crying, "Disorder is everywhere!," a phrase many of the servants take up. But the professeur merely rubs his wispy goatee, folds over and over again his ponderous cloak, and replies, "Nothing to be done, my goose is fled." Incapable of understanding why he should be more distraught over the loss of a goose than over the disappearance of a silver candelabrum she slaps him over the head with a copy of his latest book, *Tintinabula*, and he is forced to explain, poor man, hunched in his armchair and hugging his scrawny arms, that he has invited for dinner le Docteur Bruneto, an esteemed philosopher. "Aiii!" she hits him again, "And what is in my cupboard to serve him but dried lentils! I am shamed! I am degraded! I am boiled away!" She does a pro-longed dance that is less than merry but more than forlorn. She wrings a handkerchief into knots until she has nothing into which a person can nicely sneeze. Whereupon Arlequin, trusted servant, is sent to market to buy what is needed for the Docteur's soup, in particular stalks of fresh-est fennel because Bruneto, of course, is a vegetarian. On his way out the door the artful Arlequin pauses. Whenever Professeur Pantalon gives him a coin to spend for the food, Arlequin protests, "Not this, *that!*" and points to an article of the professeur's clothing. So that the professeur has to take it off and drape it over Arlequin, who starts to shiver as though he is freezing the more clothing that is laid over him. Pantalon cannot understand why Arlequin does not move off because now with the professorial clothing deco-rating his body—a silk shirt, a flowered cravat—he looks gay indeed. Nothing he gives Arlequin is sufficient, though, because the servant keeps crying, "Not this, *that!*" until finally the professeur is completely naked and Madame Leda is chasing him with a cleaver, screaming, "The soup! The soup!" at the top of her lungs. Finally Arlequin goes to market with the professeur's pointed shoe upside-down on his head.

At the market Arlequin finds Corviello selling vegetables in a huge tent. Corviello's tables are laden with baskets, all of the baskets are covered, and on top of all the basket covers there are signs: beans, tomatoes, mushrooms, fennel, that sort of thing. One sign even says, "The finest macaroni on this side of the Po," but when Arlequin asks Corviello if macaroni is indeed a vegetable Corviello begins uncontrollably to cough. Seeing that he won't get an answer to his question, Arlequin proceeds to shop for his vegetables, consulting his list. "Why don't you give me some tomatoes?" says he, and Corviello replies, "Why don't *you*?" Then Arlequin asks in the same way for squash and peppers and celeriac and pumpkin and as many other vegetables as he can think of, and for every one of these Corviello says, "Why don't *you*?" until Arlequin is at his wits' end. Then it occurs to Arlequin that maybe the thing to do is say please, so he does, whereupon Corviello becomes friendlier than friendly and informs him that because it is so late in the day all his best vegetables, in fact, are sold, except—"But what?" the servant is shaking from head to toe, "What do you have for me to cook as dinner?" "Why, *Pinocchio*, of course!" Corviello cries, tweaking Arlequin by the nose and making a play upon the Italian word for fennel, which is *finocchio*. "What's Pinocchio, pray?" says the servant, and Corviello, winking at the audience, says it's not unlike *Puccini*, holding aloft a shriveled and very unappetizing *zucchini*. Then Corviello offers *Potato*, showing off a leaking tomato; *Persichetti*, displaying some quite droopy *spaghetti*; and so on, until Arlequin snatches the fennel with great desperation and runs off.

With his sack of fennel slung over a shoulder Arlequin walks in corkscrew fashion until finally he's lost. He comes to a corner with a signpost that points in four directions: east says, "Destruction"; west says, "Devastation"; north says, "Disaster"; south says, "Decay." Under each word the servant stands bemused, folding his hands first one way and then another. Then, "I'll wait," says he, "until things look more propitious." He sits against the wall of a shop that looks very much like the enterprise of a cobbler, his hat pulled down over his eyes, snoring madly. Sure enough the beautiful Columbine comes out and discovers him sleeping. Her peachy hands fly up in thrilled surprise, and she flutters all around him like a timid butterfly, inspecting him from every angle with her almond eyes. He awakes. Seeing her gazing at him he leaps to his feet: "Oh my lady, forgive me for sleeping against this house of yours, but I have lost my way and indeed I am weary of fruitlessly searching." She throws a curious look at him, executes a polite yawn and answers, "Do not trouble yourself to worry that you are trespassing, because *he* will not mind." Arlequin: "He, my lady? Oh, forgive that I was so vulgar as to be snoring like a boar when first you should have seen me." Columbine: "There is absolutely nothing for you to be ashamed of. *He* will not have heard." Arlequin: "He again! Oh do not forsake me, dear lady, but tell me to my face of whom you speak." She looks at him but does not unfasten her persimmon lips, she only casts her eyes innocently over the shiny surface of his pink and green cap whereupon he decides to entice her confidence by tickling himself to death:

he tickles his ribs, he tickles his feet, he tickles underneath his arms, he tickles with a giant feather on the bridge of his nose, but Columbine does not speak, even though by now Arlequin is in hysterics and has turned quite as blue as a squid. Finally Arlequin falls to his knees: "Columbine! Columbine! You are the fair lady of my dreams!" At this she swoons as though afflicted with a great pain. "Woe! Woe! Only *he* may speak my name! And now, all is done with me!" Arlequin is quite prepared at this instant to throw himself into fire to know the identity of the rogue who has intimidated her so, but such a gesture is unnecessary, as the leaded window of the gable over his head is thrown open and a puffy face bellows its own blood-chilling introduction: "*Scaramouche!*"

"Papa!!" cries the startled young man, falling happily into Scaramouche's arms, and for his part the portly cobbler wets his whiskers with a flagon of Armagnac and winks, "Sooo! You have taken a fancy to my little serving maid." Immediately he draws the lovers together with profuse gesticulations and, moving Arlequin aside for a good whisper, promises to help him secure the hand of the gentle Columbine. He proposes, in point of fact, to act as go-between to carry love messages between the two young people who, after all, hardly know one another. "I," says Arlequin, "have only one message, and that is: Dearest Columbine, will you marry me?" "Ohhh, I will carry that as swiftly as a hummingbird,"

Scaramouche replies, "but for yourself you must promise me that until I bring the lady's answer back you will stand on this very spot and count backward with your eyes closed from 1000." While Arlequin stands counting, Scaramouche goes off pretending to look for Columbine, who is right in front of him brushing her hair. He mounts the stairs to her room at the top of the house and rummages everywhere, calling, "Where are youuuuuu?" apparently despondent that he cannot find her. Then he goes into the bathroom, still rummaging, and to the kitchen; to the salon and to the studio where there are half-finished boots everywhere; always crooning for Columbine, but to no avail. Then, presto!, whom does he discover outside in the street but—yes!—Columbine, exactly where she has been sitting all along. Isn't he overjoyed! Absolutely overcome with delirium! But now—he cannot remember why. Arlequin, still counting backward and pretending obediently to know nothing of what is happening, cannot help worrying that Scaramouche will forget his errand, so he holds his breath. "Dear Columbine, I knew I had something to say to you," says Scaramouche, meanwhile, scratching his head, "but what could it have been?" Arlequin is turning as purple as rhubarb. "Ah! It is a message! A message from Monsieur Arlequin!" Arlequin breathes easy. "But—what could the message have been?" Arlequin breathes faster again, moaning at every even number he passes and wailing at every odd. "Ah yes, something to do with marriage!" Arlequin breathes easy. "But what to do with marriage, what?" And so on. Until Scaramouche has finally asked Columbine the question and received her answer (the obvious one) and gone off searching everywhere for Arlequin—in the attic, in the bath, in the kitchen, turning everything upside down, "Arlequin, where aaaaaaare youuuuuuu?" Presto, he finally discovers the flustered lover all the way down to number 57. But now, although Scaramouche tries to remember Columbine's answer he cannot, for the life of him, succeed. Instead he recollects what color dress she was wearing. Then the number of brushstrokes she took through her hair. Then the color of the unfinished boots on the bench in the studio. Then the lambent amethyst color of her eyes. He draws this out so far, indeed, that Arlequin pisses in his pants with eagerness just before he gets to the number 1— whereupon Scaramouche, all at once remembering exactly what Mademoiselle Columbine did say, refuses strictly to repeat it until Arlequin begins all over again at 1000 and safely gets to the bottom. Sometimes this game is called "Love Made Large."

Escaping from the wiles of Scaramouche, Columbine brings Arlequin home to be introduced to her father, Professeur Polichinelle. This gentleman is engaged taking a painting lesson from the master, Mezzetinto. "Painting is very easy," Mezzetinto confides, "The sky is always blue, a horse is always brown, a woman is always pink—if she is looking at a man—and a tree is always exactly as green as a frog. Just look!" He points through a window at a huge oak tree, under which a man is practising drawing his rapier. "That," says Professeur Polichinelle to his daughter, "is the greatest fool on the face of the earth, Docteur Bruneto, who has so little inside his head he doesn't even need to cover it with a hat." There was nothing, indeed, upon the balding surface of the man's scalp but the blowing wind. Professeur Polichinelle has become worked up about Bruneto and is ready, moreover, to provide a long and categorical list of the Docteur's many faults when Mezzetinto interrupts him with a cry, "Come quickly, I am afraid!" Jumping away from his easel, Mezzetinto is singing and squealing at once, indeed, "Come quickly, I am afraid of this *ladybug*," and Polichinelle has to come and pick up a pretty amber thing no bigger than the head of a pin and deposit it gently outside the window. Then, pinching himself, Mezzetinto screams, "Come quickly, I am afraid of this *leech*," and Polichinelle has to extract something from the inside of the painter's britches and leave it outside as well. In this fashion Mezzetinto obtains the professeur's help ridding himself of a caterpillar, a house-fly, a robin's egg, a twig, a tube of cadmium yellow, a copy of *The Pensive Child* by Sforzetto, a piece of yeast bread in the pocket of his shirt, and a whistle you can't blow.

"My dear, esteemed, admirable Professeur Polichinelle," says Arlequin, "Kindly, honorable, revered and worthy, uplifted Polichinelle, exalted Polichinelle, noble Polichinelle, unsurpassable Polichinelle—How can it be that Docteur

Bruneto is a man with no brains in his head at all? Why, even this very evening I am engaged to cook for him a stew of fennel that will surpass anything cooked in this part of the world. And my master, Professeur Pantalon, has nothing but the greatest respect for his intelligence and his delicate wit. If he is as great a fool as you say he is, he won't know enough to appreciate the food I cook for him and then my master will be dishonored!" Professeur Polichinelle wishes to be nothing but helpful so he gives Arlequin a quantity of raw horseradish to simmer in the stew, saying, "Even a horse in a stable who knows nothing about fancy cooking will appreciate a dish that's full of this." When Arlequin gets back home he knocks on the door and Pantalon answers. Arlequin takes Pantalon for a servant and says, "You, go bring me Professeur Pantalon!" whereupon Pantalon feigns outrage and cries, "If you want Pantalon I will certainly fetch him but go back and knock again," which Arlequin does several times always receiving the same reply. By sunset Arlequin has gained admittance to the house. "I don't know about this business of the horseradish," Pantalon says, "but you're the cook, so do what you think best." While Arlequin is busy in the kitchen stirring his pot Pantalon and Leda are busy offstage throwing catcalls, such as, "Heavens, it's raining through the roof!" or "The cow is loose!" or "Arlequin has a teabag in his pants!" Docteur Bruneto arrives for his dinner in a coach drawn by a mule.

Bruneto, desiring to make privacy with the robust Madame Leda, challenges Pantalon with questions aimed at making him run out of the room to search for the answers, but every time Bruneto poses such a question Pantalon replies instead, "*About that, no knowledge exists.*" "What is the tallest tree in Belgium?" "*About that, no knowledge exists.*" "What do you put with gum tragacanth and ginger to cure a hernia?" "*About that, no knowledge exists.*" "What was the name of Attila the Hun's grandmother's sister's goatkeeper?" "*No knowledge exists.*" And so on. Pantalon thoroughly stumps Bruneto until Bruneto asks, "What is the composition of snow?" Now this question strikes Pantalon as a deliciously obscure one, to which an answer indeed exists in a book he keeps locked in a drawer in his chamber, so he runs out to find it and in his absence Bruneto proceeds to pinch Madame Leda's curves and to giggle most obscenely with her. At which point Arlequin dishes out the fennel soup. When they eat it, Bruneto is taken with a fit of gasping and Madame Leda becomes amorous. "I can't find the answer," says Pantalon, returning, "but you will discover, Bruneto, that the air is easier to breathe outside," and with that he ejects the docteur into the street and leaps upon Madame Leda himself. Arlequin now supposes that Pantalon and Leda have been thrown into a transport because of a faulty recipe so he throws some salt into the soup and, breaking in between them as they writhe on the floor beneath the table, whispers, "*Taste this!*" inserting a spoon into each of their mouths. They only entwine more rigorously so he adds pepper and tries "*Taste this!*" again, and once again with sugar and once again with honey and once again with bay leaves and once again with cumin until he has gone through all of the spices in the kitchen, bottle by bottle, and the soup now tastes so horrid both Pantalon and Leda have to rush out to water the garden. "It would have been better," mumbles Arlequin, "to eat goose."

Scaramouche convinces Mezzetinto to paint a portrait of the Docteur Bruneto. This latter person, having escaped the table, has perched himself on Professeur Pantalon's veranda and is fanning his lips. But Mezzetinto drops his paints down Pantalon's well. Scaramouche bends over to reach for them and Arlequin attempts to tie a bell to the fat man's ass. Mezzetinto, meanwhile, falls asleep, muttering, curiously, "La finicula!" Scaramouche discovers what Arlequin is doing and clubs him with Mezzetinto's flaccid leg.

Bruneto proclaims bitterly that Professeur Pantalon has ordered Madame Leda to poison him by causing her servant Arlequin to lay out an inedible stew. Everyone, Pantalon, Leda, Bruneto, Scaramouche, and Mezzetinto starts calling to the servant, *"Arlequin, have you made the macaroni?"* This becomes a game. No matter what anyone says somebody else interrupts him in a very loud voice, *"Arlequin, have you made the macaroni?"* Somebody succeeds in tying the bell to

Bruneto's ass and he remains ignorant, dingling here and dangling there. Scaramouche has his moustache carefully clipped by the stuttering barber Frapozzi who says he has observed the lunatic Pierrot in the gardens staring. "Staring at what?" says Scaramouche. "At the t-t-t—" says Frapozzi, clipping the moustache. "The *what*?" "The t-t-t———" he clips some more. And the conversation goes on this way, everyone coddling Frapozzi to say what Pierrot is staring at and Frapozzi stuttering and stuttering as he clips, and clipping as he stutters, until finally it comes out, "At the t-t-t-tether!" At this Scaramouche is outraged. "What tether! There is no tether in the garden!" But everyone is beside himself laughing at Scaramouche now, because Frapozzi has cut his moustache all away and whispers at this moment into his ear, "And no t-t-t-tether in this place, either!" They all fall into rapture, guzzling wine by the bottleful and crying out, *"No tether here!"* until Scaramouche runs away.

Pantalon has, indeed, quite a marvelous garden with rows and rows of flowers, sculpted furzes, hedges lush with purple berries, manicured lawns where chipmunks sit. Here Arlequin and Columbine are reunited in the moonlight, and they whisper delirious syllables into one another's hair. Columbine: "Who is it?" Arlequin: "One who reads the catalogue of his faults by thy light." Columbine: "But your faults are tinier than fleas." Arlequin: "And your kindness in saying so is magnified, even though already it is over-whelming." Columbine: "I love you." Arlequin: "I vanish when I see you because your beauty is the entire world." Columbine: "Oh, do not vanish, for I would gaze at you until the end of time." And so on. Observing them is Pierrot. He is all in white satin, and his face is soft and sad. He walks with white feet on tiptoe upon the moonlit lawns, curling from one bush to another as the lovers, cooing, move along bathed in one another's sight. Pierrot then wanders into the rose garden, counting the number of red roses and the number of yellow ones although it is difficult to tell the difference by moonlight, and finally he contents himself by collapsing at the lovers' feet. "What is this?" says Colum-bine, lifting him up, "a kind of sweetness!" Pierrot crumples again and Arlequin says, "What is this—a kind of joy!" Pierrot, for his part, is so happy to be with the lovers that he accompanies them, henceforward, everywhere they go like a kind of shadow.

Un Ballo in Maschera

THE ONE they call Trufaldino, whose humor has touched the breast of almost every prince in Venice, is himself despondent when he is not engaged in clownery. Long lips. Dishevelled matted hair. Eyes dull as unwashed muscat grapes veiled by an army of flies. You'll see him throughout the afternoon walking the Piazza San Marco like nothing more than a beggar (though Amaril himself sent, it is rumored, payments totalling half a million crowns only last month). With a sluggishness you can spy all the way from the Lido he navigates back and forth outside the animal enclosures at Punta Sabbioni, his thick buffoon lips imitating with grievous precision the lamentable sadness of a Great Ethiopian Gorilla who's pacing in his malodorous cage and staring with moon eyes at a spot over the heads of the vain children who come to toss pepperoni at his nose. "There he goes, there goes Trufaldino," citizens mutter who pass him, "Funniest man in the north," but no, he does not, even on rare afternoons when the sun has gone wild bouncing off the gondoliers' candy poles, cast off a comedian's smile. Rumor has it lethargic antipathetic Trufaldino has a colossal mind: in his metric sombre step, with shoulders stooped under an invisible yoke, he's concocting to himself the very proportions of the universe. Who can know? On stage later it is sure that he is nothing but hilarity itself, bouncing into his net with four dozen prodigious watermelons and calling out in a voice as raucous as a morning rooster's,

> Uccellini i miei nessuno piglia
> Non mammina sera!
> La verbosa bobina abbia
> Filando in mia pancia!,

(the translation of which is quite unprintable).

Having suffered in silence the intolerable circumstance of a childhood imposed by parents whose wit hers far exceeded, Mademoiselle Celia (of peachy complexion) has resolved herself in a search for the literary life. She lets it be known far and wide—which is to say, as far to the south as the Canale del Brenta—that no suitor need press his attentions for her hand who cannot hold a place among the great bards of her city, to wit, Shakespeare, Byron, Goethe, Keats, Mme de Staël, Ruskin, Casanova and Gabriele D'Annunzio. She goes everywhere—that is to say, to a posh leather shop on the Calle della Mandola and a dilapidated caffè near the Palazzo Ducale—followed by a stooping old nurse who wheels a collapsing wooden cart laden with gilded volumes. It is autumn, the wind is blowing through the yellowing trees over at the Teatro Verde. The water is whipped up to a slight foam in the San Marco, very deep blue, almost black, with bouncing cappuccino crests. By no means optimistic about her mistress's chances of attracting the bearer of a suitable codpiece while flaunting all this textuality, the old nurse, Ruffiana by name, attempts to cloak the mouldering treatises beneath her burlap skirt as she hauls them over the rancid bricks, and to stimulate her young lady's concupiscence by playing aloud a game in which it is necessary to invoke as many as possible of the pet names for a young hero's machinery: beginning, to be sure, with banana and proceeding quite as far as potato-finger, with intermediate stops at pizzle, whizzle, jizzle, needle, purse (obscure), bat and bag, zucchini, zucchini with olives, zucchini with baby onions, damsons and dagger, ling-tickler, and yardarm. But Celia has her head above all this. She is interested only in fetching a first edition of Frazzato's *The Temptation of San Antonio in the Garden of Holy Torture*, fetching it and reading with melancholy patience while someone quite beneath acknowledgment massages the little crevices between her toes.

The canals being overcrowded Arlecchino is unable to obtain a gondola and so he establishes himself in front of the Libreria Vecchia with his arms grandiloquently posing: in this direction, in that direction, now like the anxious branches of the bambolla shrub, now like spinning fishes, once rigid as tempered spears, then pliant as newboiled tagliarini. He has invented a game, "Terror!" To wit: Here's the Lord Marfoglia punted around by two bald eunuchs; now they're passing this wonderful point of vantage of his; Arlecchino leans over to his confederate Pulcinella and bellows, indeed so that all Venezia can hear, "—Yes, *guilty!* Just precisely as guilty as *Marfoglia*, as everybody has been saying *at court!*" Old Marfoglia practically tips his boat jumping at the sound of his own name resounding from the banchina, nor is his careening heart calmed when he sees the two bedazzled rapscallions pointing, gesticulating sensuously, raising their eyebrows up to very heaven in elaborate reprehension. Marfoglia practically tips his boat three times, indeed, (What a game!) but then he's gone in a mutter under the Ponte di Paglia, and—"Terror!"—the Duca di Firenze is having his turn, in a green craft piloted by a little man all in plum red, only this time the victim makes the mistake of standing to see where the gossip's coming from and the next thing anybody knows the water's seething with his ostrich feathers which have popped out of the ducal tunic and been carried in all directions, toward China, toward Cape Bougaroun, toward Miami Beach…(Terrific game, "Terror," Arlecchino's never had so much fun with another, but tomorrow there'll be a replacement, pro forma, and again the day after that, because Arlecchino doesn't believe in anything if it's not the abrogation of every limit of the human imagination.) Pulcinella, meanwhile, quite exhausted from a day of playing the supportive role, wanders off on his own to that tiny canal that angles up past the Via Garibaldi. There, round about sunset, he sees the ardent

Celia with her old nurse disembarking from a craft that's practically water-logged. The nurse is dangling the keys to what looks like a new apartment, and, in fact, behind the two wraithlike flitting women bearers are heaving chests and sacks that could fill Amenhotep's tomb. But soon the old lady comes stumbling out, puffing, cursing, throwing up her hands, and then sixteen times she spits upon the banchina, spits to the north, spits to the south, spits in every direction two times, with her well-read young innocent gawking in horror as she hoarsely cries, "The place is haunted! I should have known! *Infestata! Infestata!*"

A magical—a terrifying—word. Report is squeezed out of Pulcinella, over cinnamon buns, by Leandro; Leandro gives it to old Cassandro; Cassandro to Pipaza, Pipaza to Scafulia, Scafulia to Terzeretto and thence by way of Mastopopo and Carracazza to the flaccid ears of mopey Trufaldino, the same Trufaldino who cannot bring himself to laugh and who is simple enough to believe everything he hears. The mob gathers with brooms and pails full of urine, with straw baskets filled with snippets of horse's mane, with linden blossoms hacked into confetti. It doesn't help at all that the old lady has gathered her wits by this time, has proclaimed quite confidently, "Of course, every house is haunted." They come storming in, they wash the whole place down, they strew whatever they're carrying on the hearth; they come back day after day for seventy-two days, hour after hour

33

singing dirges…. By this time we have found ourselves face to face with the very depths of winter and the colors have gone out of everyone's cheeks.

Old Pantalone's hung up all his wigs for good, now that the trespassing case of *Mademoiselle Celia vs. Trufaldino et alia* has been thrown out for lack of evidence. He's laid down all his portfolios. The memorabilia from his three barren marriages to his three fat wives he's stored in three bedrooms on the topmost floor of his moss-hung palazzo. He nibbles throughout the afternoons on the curlicues of lemon peel a Nubian majordomo slivers off for him with a sharpened ivory. Though agents present him with entertainments from the five continents—dancing bears, dancing reindeer, dancing Peruvian dwarfs—he falls asleep. Pantalone has a daughter, mystic Flaminia. She has the enormity of a discus-thrower, and coal-flaming eyes. But Flaminia has been blessed with a voice as yet uncompared; rare as Carthaginian quail or as the fabled waters of the clear spring of Rud-Mehran. Emperors have fallen upon their bellies to hear what she sings (even after the sumptuous luncheons given on Thursdays in the pine groves out at Malamocco). Yes, emperors have covered their mouths with their hands. And now Flaminia is singing at midnight, from her launch on the Laguna, she is singing from *Cosi fan tutti*, the aria that begins "Fra gliamplessi, in pochi istanti," and her father is wakened in tears from his sleep. No stars, nothing but darkness. She cannot be seen in the darkness without moon, her voice floats into Venezia as the very waters do.

Sireno, son of Pantalone. He cannot stop laughing, a cruel twist on the old tale. He has never stopped laughing as long as anyone can remember. But it can hardly be said joy has ever roused him, not even at this moment when the loon voice of his sister is wafted along the canals, since in sad fact the smile is pasted upon his features like a scar. Flaminia sings out of happiness, Sireno is silent out of grinning despond. Kind Pantalone is beside himself with care, he has tried everything to help the boy. A man of uncountable riches, he has brought spices from Mandalay for his son's administration (illicit potions having been prescribed by the city's ancient eminent clowns) and he has paid jugglers from unreachable Hispanica to flip their colors in a pantomime of exquisite sorrow—but to no avail. The old doctor, Cassandro, is consulted. (When he breathes people think they hear shuffling cabbage leaves.) He is quite explicit. "This is well-known. This is often seen. When he reaches his twenty-first year your son will be freed from this plague of laughter." But no—every year until Sireno is thirty the old doctor has to be consulted. Pantalone is desperate, he sends far and wide to receive anyone and anything that can be regarded as a cure. Sireno will barely touch his food for the magnanimity of the rictus. Moreover, his unrelenting expression of delirium brings instantaneous agony to the faces of all who meet him. Pantalone sends out his most trusted servant, Cola, with orders to find a cure or die trying.

"—Oh, but sir!" Mademoiselle Celia tosses a protest, as the hand of the bearded beggar who had been asking for gorgonzola money slides between her indignant kneecaps. Can it be the hand belongs to misfortuned Trufaldino? Can it be that grasping it, Celia finds her hand taken hold of in turn, and drawn to the man's drooping cheek, which is o'erflooded with the moisture of despair. Can it be that they sit upon an embankment (where slowly the water churns), brushing the present from one another's faces with their kisses…?

The body of an old man is dragged from the Grand Canal by the police, dressed in magenta capes. Somebody identifies him as Cola, aged manservant of the great retired magistrate Pantalone (the one who got Bastarucozzo off, when it looked like they'd hang him three times over). This Cola has apparently dropped over the Ponte dei Sospiri where, earlier in the evening, some boys chasing a fat little bambina toward the pepper market saw him spying on lovers passing in gondolas beneath. Conclusion: his legs must have given out as he depended over the luscious choreographies, and finally he couldn't swim an inch. The water there is as purple as

36

ink, and as final. But how, some wanted to know, did all this become evident? All this became evident because when the old women at the pepper market whispered what had been going on (one of the boys was wearing very tight pants) the fat little bambina's mother slapped her silly, so the pullet went squealing to the police, who proceeded to round up the boys, who couldn't stop leaking giggles, and who finally spilled the beans on Cola, whom, indeed, they'd been watching surreptitiously for hours while they masturbated in dark triangles of shadow. In cases of this sort gondolieri are always cooperative, so it wasn't difficult to discover that two of the lovers who'd been bobbing first up and then down the canal (entertaining Cola in a veritable tango) had been licking tears off one another's cheeks (an odd detail worth noting in the record) and that on landing finally along the Riva del Carbon they'd been met by a figure in a black robe with a candle who said the forbidden word, "Porfiria" before disappearing under the Rialto like a bundle of stolen goods. On police orders a trace is instigated. The chief himself, Zubini, looks into the whole affair, from the very beginning, and decides there must be a single unifying theory that will sew every nitty piece of evidence to every other, filthy Trufaldino's secret poems, Mademoiselle Celia's entirely questionable relationship with her aged nurse, seditious Pantalone's offbeat children, even the tumbling scarlet and golden leaves which seem to be collecting on the rooftops in curious, half-intelligible patterns. Then there's Porfiria, what's Porfiria?, is it a place, is it a code? Zubini herds all the suspects into the music room of the Palazzo

37

Pestarini where the floor's inlaid with walnut wood. Marfoglia himself is paid to handle the catering, he's got wagons full of spinach. While the chief is off doing his formulations with an assistant who claims to be able to derive intelligence from the droppings of a vulture, that provocative goofball Arlecchino is brought in to provide entertainment since tomorrow, after all, will be the first day of winter, season of transformations. (Sireno and Trufaldino are already busy behind a screen trying on masks…)

Once upon a time (the wisecracker says), in the great city of Sonnambula, which spreads itself under the moonlight like a thousand tiaras, there was a child with an obscene spot, a spot the color of raspberries, on the middle of his forehead. (Polite cough. Polite sneeze.) All of the doctors were consulted, even Cassandro himself, and for nothing. For days the spot grew redder, redder and hotter. Rumor of the spot spread around the city and people came from far and wide to get a glimpse. (Two polite sneezes, three polite coughs.) Ritually at evensong the child was bathed in a fountain that springs from a vault beneath the holy Church of San Lorenzo il Mendicanto, bathed and dipped and dipped and dunked from head to foot right side up and upside down. Niente, nulla, zero. (Zero!) The mother tore her hair. The father tore his shirt and beat his thighs with the thongs from off his feet. Public swathers wrapped the child in purple organdy and then in ceremonial white and finally in turmeric yellow, but the spot only grew redder and more inexplicable. (Cosi!) Then poof, suddenly, on a Monday morning, a Monday before an important Tuesday, (the Tuesday of elocutions), when no one in Sonnambula could have been prepared exactly for this, the spot on the child's head was gone. Poof. (Cosi! Cosi! Cosi!) Bells, a thousand bells. No one could dream of the explanation. No one could dream how, no one could dream why. A mask thrown off, a mask dissolved in the liquid of time. ("Una maschera dissoluta nel fluido del tempo!") Arlecchino's quite ready to finish his story, but impossible—the chief of police has come back in maschera and ordered the music; now he's very much caught up in the dance (his livid teeth strung with spinach from Marfoglia's tarts), he's twisting around as though it's been decided the death of old Cola's impenetrable. Soon enough, quite according to form, the liveried servants pass around, raising mirrors to all our masked faces, wily Zubini guised as a maiden of easy virtue, gorgeous Flaminia with the voice unearthly now silent behind the facade of a fortune-teller, Trufaldino as Sireno smiling once and for all, Sireno as Trufaldino at last, and ecstatically, approaching a succulent grimace of despair...

A wind in the street is shuffling through the fading chestnut trees.

Henry or Henry

{ French Disease }

AUGUST THE 9th, 1546, precisely four hundred years before I was born, at 10:30 o'clock of the forenoon: the Palace of Hampton Court, south and west-by-south-west of London after eight green meanders of the chilly Thames. Whitechapel workmen are installing along the King's Stair a device upon pulleys, with weights and ropes and ballasts, and with six gears, for hoisting to his great bed, within a smallish yellow room adjacent the Audience Chamber, the ailing, flatulent, bloated, adamant eighth Henry of England; whose hour of agony without good speed approaches; and half of whose half dozen wives have gone before him without grace; whose flaccid skin has yellowed and browned, and whose teeth have rotted, and whose eyes have puffed, and whose fingers have gone stiff and vibrant and rubicose, and whose knees have locked, and whose tongue has gone pussy white, and whose gaunt neck in every hour blossoms with a fetter of ermine. "French Disease," have pronounced his physicians, one of whom, Docteur Bruneto from the Continent, quotes in a blithe wheeze Girolamo Fracastoro's recent *Syphilis sive Morbus Gallicus*:

Muse, what causes presided at the origin of this scourge so long wrapped in the darkness of nothing? Was it imported among us from those new worlds which were discovered by the brave mariners of Spain beyond the unknown seas of the Western world? Have we received from those far countries the germ where it is said it has reigned as sovereign master from all eternity, numbering as many victims as there are inhabitants? Is it true that introduced, in that manner, among us it was then spread throughout Europe by means of commercial relations? Is it true that it was born weak and obscure, to increase its force a hundred fold later on as it extended its ravages and invaded, little by little, the entire universe? Such as once, springing from a badly extinguished focus which an imprudent shepherd left in the country, a single spark sufficed to start a conflagration; the fire first slumbers and insidiously spreads in the grass, then bursts out with fury; the flame, fed by the fuel, then raises itself in threatening tongues, devours on its passage the fields and prairies, fires forests which fall with a crash, and throws afar off baleful lights on sky and earth.

Other chirurgeons have given other pronouncements, typically, "Cirrhosis." Others, "Gout." And still others, for have there not been hundreds of opinions, "Extensive but Indefinable Morbidity." The bedchamber is bloated, the bed cramped, with diagnoses. Soon the bedchamber will be removed to the ground floor altogether, and the royal days

44

will be an uninterrupted fluence of blood coughed up, and His Majesty will be carried from here to there on wheels, and out of torpor His Majesty will virtually cease to sign (in that hobby of his) death warrants. Into a waking sleep he will drop, and his great royal organ will become shrivelled and blacken, and he will certainly hallucinate upon the corpses he has sent away without coffins. He will remember, upon his deathbed, for months, his drama-life; nor will die for one hundred and seventy-two wracking days; and now with curiosity observes erected that machinery for hoisting and dropping him, is watching the way the men obsessively wipe their hands upon their smocks as they work, and mutter with their eyes screwed up. He has begun himself to mutter considerably. He is muttering hoarsely, "Atahualpa...seized by Cortez! Magellan...dismembered! Holbein...a vapor, my precious Holbein! The Inca...garoted! And my Boleyn, my darling Boleyn...O, what has become of my Boleyn..."

{ Three Divertimenti to the Glory of the Tomato }

Do you know, reader, what this man witnessed in his one lifetime, merely at table? When he was a child he had never imagined these things, but first with his knife and later with his fork he placed into his mouth, before any other man in Europe, slivers of turkey sent by way of the Spanish conquistadors (who had seen men of the New World devouring, it is true!, slugs, tadpoles, winged ants, water flies, white

45

worms, larvae of various insects, and iguanas); and, too: tomatoes (sieved, sliced, pickled), avocados (purée of, slivered, with meat of crab), papayas (whole, juiced), vanilla (sirop, essence, ground bean, pudding), chocolate (heated, chilled, grated with pepper), sweet potatoes (sweet potatoes stewed with prunes and raisins, mashed sweet potatoes, sweet potatoes gratinéed with almonds and coriander), green beans (steamed, cut on the bias, stewed with fennel and roux), paprika (of Spain, of Hungary, of the Balearics), sweet oranges (with pulp and without pulp liquified, sectioned with berries of the pomegranate), potatoes (roasted, mashed, boiled, fried, grated, turned into cakes, turned into pancakes, turned into puddings, turned into pouches for holding lardons, champignons, suet custards), maize (whole, dried, flour of, made into flat cakes), savoy cabbage (boiled, broiled), broccoli (with cheese, with onions, with giblets, with macedoine of hare), globe artichokes (green, golden, russet, with melted fat and mince of garlic), truffles (of Perigord, of Dussac, of Bastignole, slivered thickly, slivered thinly, upon soups, upon omelettes), barley, chickpeas, wheat (ground and bleached and baked a thousand ways), the flesh of cows. No Englishman had eaten the flesh of cows. He came to invent a dish with slices of papaya and shavings of chocolate, and a dish with sweet oranges and avocados, and a luscious, peppery stew of the flesh of cows with carrots and potatoes…. He wrote three divertimenti for wind orchestra to the glory of the tomato, did he not!

{ Cold Shower }

At this very moment that effete sop Amaril is swooning in
the dells of Sopwith Trembling, while the consort of
Boreham perform Henry's second divertimento. Is it the
fluted hemidemisemiquavers or the blushing cheek of Mademoiselle Lalia, whose fingers flip upon her gauzy skirts
and tug at her lacy bodice? Will he have to run out before
the cadenza for a cold shower, mmmmnn?

{ Oute of ye Frying Panne and into ye Fyr }

Pipicastranzo!, daylight has seen the publication of *The Prov-
erbs of John Heywood*. All around the nasturtium garden fellows are going mad upon girls, wild fellows upon wild girls,
bending their feathers and flipping their noses up and down,
twirling and swirling and unfurling. Scarlet dresses, golden
tresses, gilding and beguiling and chartreuse ribbons and
blue satins as deep as the sea! What a sound!: shivers of
hautboys and hooting rauschpfeifen and douçaines and
kortholts and crumhorns and cornamuses and bagpipes and
shawms, soprano, alto, tenor and bass shawms, and flutes
and gemshorns too. Trills and shivers and arcane ascen-
sions and strident configurations. Porcine spinsters bending over with mulligrums, oi! We have Ardenzio and Columbine and Cassandro and Leandro, Harlequin and
Mezzetinto, Flaminia and Pulcinello flinging themselves
upon one another, and flinging, too, the wisdoms of John

47

Heywood, to be sure. To wit: "Ther be more thinges to a marriage than four bare fete in a bedde." Or, "Looke before you lepe." Or then, "Beggars shoulde no chosers be." And, "All's welle that endes welle." And, too, "Welle mite a man bringe hors to watter but cannot make him drinke." As well, "Butter wolde not melte in her mouthe." With his copy of the book Pulcinello has gone quite off the edge: "Ye fatte is in ye fyr. Haf a lof is better than non. It's an ill winde that blows no goodde. One swallowe maketh not the summer. One guid tourne deserveth another." Quotes Columbine in Ardenzio's blushing ear, "Better layt than never." And he to her, "Love me, love my dogge." And she to Flaminia, who's grasping for an apronful of strawberries, "Rome was not bilte in a day." And Amaril, when he sees that the fingers of the great Lord Scaramouche have found their way under his nether-straps: "Oute of ye frying panne and into ye fyr!" Harlequin, poor sod, is standing on his head with happiness, oblivious of what is soon to come.

{ Salvation }

Let Harlequin, poetic soul that he is, encounter the engaging, if not enchanting, and certainly endearing, Henry Howard, otherwise known as the second Henry of the court (although, to be sure, there are Henries oozing from the brickwork), and a man with many enemies. It is the 2nd of December. There is no snow. The winds are still lush. The King is rapidly declining and sees no one but his physicks, who say nothing. Harlequin is in a fit of despair, having failed spectacularly to raise the royal spirits either by standing on his head and whistling; or by juggling sixteen red balls; or by quoting words that begin with Q; or by coining bawdy rhymes; by wearing an omelette like a hat upon his head; by pretending to make love to Columbine in French; by playing the game called "The Happy Bargain" where he trades Pulcinello a salami for six strands of pearls; by blowing into a lute and trying to strum a bass recorder; by using one of those newfangled doodahs with prongs, that the King is so proud of for stabbing beef, as a utensil for tickling the armpits of Mezzetinto and Scapino. Nothing has worked and Harlequin figures he'll be the next one up on the scaffold, where you have to make a little speech saying how ashamed you are before they lop off your head with a blunt axe and hold it up with the eyes still popping to get a rise out of that crowd half bored to death. But suddenly: salvation, in the form of a perfectly gay young man, with flaming hair, and a purple jerkin, and a lute, and a book, and light in his eyes, strolling by the river…

{ Come, Jest for Me }

"Come, jest for me," says Henry Howard with a lacy look. "Come, come, and in my circle you will surely taste the delights of the civilized world." Harlequin answers, "Could I stand on my head beneath the balcony of a princess and blow farts at the moon?"

49

{ Serious, Studious, and Devoted Men }

"Look!" says the Archbishop of Canterbury, Thomas Cranmer, about whom more anon. He's nothing if not a pedant, as gray as a flatfish with the chin of a boarhound. "There, walking by the river, that fey and insipid young genius, Henry Howard, whose vices are without number and whose nauseating prostrations do mock all that is lifted up by serious, studious, and devoted men. And who is that in silks behind him, flinging fettucine? Mark, but a head shall fall. Mark, but we shall discover!"

{ di-DA/ di-DA/ di-DA/ di-DA/ di-DA }

Henry Howard admits to Harlequin he's wronged the King a hundred ways and is terrified he'll be the next one up on the scaffold, where you have to make a little speech saying how remorseful you are before they lop off your head with a blunt axe and hold it up with the eyes still popping to get a rise out of that dirty crowd half bored to death. "O Woe!" he cries, but then, miracle of miracles, he composes, in a fourme as yet on Engelische shors unkenned, this:

> Coulde Ich but say how faire Ik loved my cyng
> Nor yet be strened in bondes of descontente,
> Yif in the scabbèd wode with rightwis ringe
> I'd seled a royall troth and freedom spente;

To see by greater passion dutes wuyde,
Or counte meself a capitain proude of men,
Or dele a fyry matchless blowe in pruyde
Without a pause to wundor hwy or whenne;

And had for tresors all the voutes of golde
And all your maydens tresses red and wilde,
Or wittes brethles Gestour swete and olde
And titel, truste and treuthe as Henry's childe;

Thenne my sharpe feres wolde softe as ripels be
Wher on kinde sandes outepours a bestial see.

"What what what?" says Harlequin, touching his jester's
stick (Gestour-stikke) to his forehead. "Fourteen lines, do
I hear? Why, three quatrains and a couplet! And each line,
gorblimey!, built of—what!—five (count 'em!) iambic feet?"
If this is not the beginning of the importation to England of
the sonata ("The Italian sonnet," explains Howard, fiddling
with the locket that's dangling from his neck), we don't
know what is. More: "This newe kinde of writynge," says
he, "di-DA/ di-DA/ di-DA/ di-DA/ di-DA, I call ye blanke
vers." Harlequin puts up his fingers to pinch off his nose:
"Absolutely disgusting, positively revolting. Quintes-
sentially unpublishable." But there's no time for this. Tomorrow or tomorrow or tomorrow Henry Howard will be
arrested for high treason, because, among other things,
somebody's noticed the King's arms sewn on his under-
wear. And, poopoo, he has a hunger. Babbling his assur-

ance that someone someday somewhere will appreciate his poetry for what it is, he scurries off to his estate in Little Snoring for a dinner of luscious Norfolk cauliflower. Harlequin, meanwhile, takes this opportunity to extemporize:

Ye boye wych hath twin pyples 'pon his noos
Can never finde a boteled beere to drinke.
But whenne he dumpes his garbage doun ye sinke
It lekes upon his cneo-hoos and his toos.
So of he flys to kissen a wench's titte
And take a bite wher dogges love to sniffe
While she doth squatte upon fair yonder cliffe
To souke his peach from tawny skinne to pitte.

Ye moral of this tale is simply seyne
By all who crepyng lough do nose ye streete
Whenne proude before them walkes a cyng or quene—
Be stille before you crave a forein trete
And keepe your heed intact and vertu clene.
Ye bravest falle for candi much too sweete.

{ Coup de Grâce }

It's New Years 1547, hoop-de-doo! Henry Howard, the Earl of Surrey, is damp and anxious in the Tower of London, far too optimistically awaiting lily-wristed Mistress Columbine with a plate of letters from his wife and sister to the effect that, in his cavern of misery, the King has seen the light of lovingkindness and signed documents to reprieve him; but, alas, the Lady hasn't come at all (because lusty Scapino, of the tumbling moustache, having caught a whiff of her handmaiden's goose-liver unguent, has attacked with all ten fingers, thus obstructing the combing out of the official tresses). Hard luck. But worse, much worse: rumor has spread through the Court, and been sucked up by Sir Richard Southwell, odious nitpicker, that Harlequin, coxcomb-and-balls to Surrey, has origins in, of all places, Italy. Coup de grâce. Sixteen years after Wolsey's death it is still treasonable to employ an Italian jester. Poor Harlequin, alias Arlecchino, unemployed again, what can he do, *che cosa fare*? And as to Surrey: he's for it, signed, sealed and delivered, and his father to boot, Thomas Howard, Duke of Norfolk, and if the King will have his way, before things are done, the entire Howard family as well. Henry Howard, you're so pretty, like an anemone trampled in the city. He opens the locket that's hanging around his neck and gazes at the little etching Holbein did for him of Henry Fitzroy, sweet Henry, Prince Henry, dead these eleven years, brother-in-law, friend, confidant, you name it, O sweet bliss of Henries!, but a Henry, alas, quite out of the picture. Bells sound in the distance and bells sound in the distance and bells sound. Somebody outside the door of his cell passes swirling in a gay conversation, "I'm telling you, it's Tintoretto or Correggio, I'm telling you. Tintoretto or Correggio. And if——" Henry Howard clasps his hands together for courage, tells himself everything will be all right: the wise and compassionate Archbishop of Canterbury will save him.

53

{ "We have all the evidence." }

The Archbishop of Canterbury is sipping his Haut Brion
in the golden, lintel-burnishing afternoon light, thinking of
the wormish turnings of the diseased spirit of his predeces-
sor, Thomas Wolsey, and, by antithesis, of his own lucid
and ecclesiastical pristineness. "It is not a matter for con-
sideration," he whispers, "that Henry Howard is the bringer
to England of the sonata Italiana, or that in only a few years
a certain William Shakespeare, using this very form, will
exemplify unto all ages our English tongue, or that the man
is young and robust and of good temper in this age of cat-
erwauling and ladder-climbing and lies. He has committed
treason. We have the documents. We have all the evidence.
But the head that wears the crown doth daily rot. And now
it is only a question of which Henry will be the first to die.
Surely one will philosophize upon the carcass of the other."

{ A Ceremonial Tea Party }

The Countess of Frangipane has given a ceremonial tea
party, to which Henry Howard the Earl of Surrey has had
to send his regrets, but at which Pulcinello is awkwardly
playing the dulcimer and Harlequin, standing upon his head,
is morosely sending up farts. The purpose is to honor the
fifteenth anniversary of the invention, by Count Cesare Frangipani of Rome (no relative at all, none whatever, tut tut
tut), of an exquisite almond pastry to which she is abso-

54

lutely—ooo-la-la-la—addicted. On silver plates she's got mounds and mounds of these frangipani, and her fingertips are quite pink with pleasure at having passed so many to her bulbous lips. Somebody—it's that idiot Pantalone—says, in just one year it will be possible to have another tea party to celebrate the fifteenth anniversary of the double boiler, *il bagno maria* after Signior Maria de Cleofa of Padua; and a year after that to celebrate at a third tea party the invention of the pieshell by a charwoman in Kent, Maggie Scamswit; and then, after a recess of merely a year, to have a tea party for the celebration of the fifteenth anniversary of the invention of flyswatters by the Bishop of Lower Trelewney; and, and, and, and, and, tut tut. This game is called nothing less than "Happy Anniversary"; "In twelve years—!" calls Pandolfo, tugging his earlobes, "In twelve years——!" and at this moment Amaril is delicately placing a frangipane upon the tongue of squirming Lalia, who makes a sound like that of strutting pigeons. They go off together to sample more frangipani in the library where in their exertions they manage to bump from a waist-high shelf a first edition of *De Revolutionibus Orbium Coelestium*, 1543, by that unhappy Pole Mikolaj Kopernik. The cover flips open upon Amaril's crumpled silk pants and he sees, in a faint hand, the broken phrase "À ma plus chère Comt—"; then someone else has inscribed, very tidily, "May 24, 1543. Signed by Copernicus while dying." The lovers position themselves in the fading pink light with a plate of frangipani and make revolution after revolution after revolution.

In the Bureau of Condemnations, meanwhile, a great furor has erupted because it turns out that in order to have someone's head legally separated from his body it is necessary first to specify in a sealed death warrant the precise identity of the criminal corpse so as to mitigate against all contingency of error. Involved is the accurate enunciation of the accused's full and legal name, in this case:

> Henry Malcolm Richard Hewlett Droigneur (pron. Drowner) Maithewson Voyley (pron. Varley) Stroughms (pron. Strums) Blakenish Vincent de Leuvre (pron. Delaver) Howard, seventeenth Earl of Surrey, heir to the Dukedom of Norfolk.

But it is also a queer case that the lethal document must contain the precise date of corporeal birth, a requirement that has caused no end of consternation since of Henry Howard, in short, the commencement was not recorded. "Sometime in 1517," says Pantalone, always the one who'll try to be helpful, "I know because I remember I was having a couple of teeth removed, and—" There's a voice from another part of the great chamber. "April 27. It must be April 27. It is known to have been in April, and it surely couldn't have been before the 26th or later than the 28th, because of—" Someone recollects that the irises hadn't yet bloomed, or was it the roses, and the irises never bloom until the 1st of June (while the roses bloom somewhat later),

so it couldn't have been April 27, because there was a bou-
quet of irises, or was it roses? This horticultural rant makes
old Pandolfo remember somebody's paean to a rosebush:

> Hast thou, in anguisse, oute-weven, of wery nose
> Sunke depe in draughtes of colde despeir and glome?
> Give but a glance the frayel herte of a rose
> And finde salvation's blome.

Voices and voices and voices. The Countess of Frangipane
(no relation at all, tut tut, to Count Cesare Frangipani of
Rome) is quite certain Mary Howard, Henry Howard's
mater, was in her late confinement in August of 1517, or
could it have been September? Because the new silks had
arrived from the Continent, those wonderful silks, particu-
larly the mauve fleur-de-lys taffeta with the magenta shadowing upon the silver leaves, or was it the silver shadowing
on magenta leaves?, which means he was probably born
September something-or-other. Or was his mother's name
Elizabeth, Mary's sister, or was it Mary's cousin?, in which
case it was February, when the little marzipan storks were
decorating cakes all over London? Marzipan is so very *comme
il faut!* And then Pulcinello is blowing farts upon farts upon
farts and saying, "January, January, I remember everything."
And Amaril is trying to unfasten something of Lalia's while
she's whining, "This is most, most, most unfortunate!,"
and he can't, he can't, he can't move fast enough, his silks
are stained in a cloud of frenzy. Cranmer's man says, "We
have procured every document. Put May 1, 1517!" but Sir

57

Richard Southwell, who is responsible for the prosecution, seems to believe the date must have been sometime in late November or early December. "I will have him to death," says he. "I will eat him with jurisprudence." Madame Leda stands in an ante-room stirring a tea of parsnips and peony blossoms which will be very good with some honey if only they can get the honey shortage cleared up. Parsnip and peony blossom and plumskin tea. And poor Harlequin, flopped hopelessly in the rock garden, his silks all drawn, a smile coldly etched upon his quivering face.

{ Henry Howard, Please }

Parsnip and peony blossom and plumskin tea is the last thing on busy Pierrot's mind as he counts the pears dangling from the espaliering upon the south wall. He's keeping records for the Archbishop of Canterbury, who likes to have records of everything. Somebody's called it Warham's Revenge, who knows why. Revenge upon whom, for what? And who's Warham? Now, finishing the espaliered pears and also the canker vines and also the silver plate, he'll move on to catalogue the hairs in the goatees of all the little beardlings who cling unctuously to the margins of the Court, Fisher, Parr, Hoby, Elyot, that lisping Henry Howard. Henry Howard, please. The Earl of Surrey? Hello, where is Henry Howard the Earl of Surrey to be found? Time for the Evaluation of the Goatee, please. And answers to many questions, such as, "When did you first snicker at the little circular jokes of an Italian?" Pierrot keeps records, and then he keeps records about the records and still other records about where all these other records are kept.

{ Quite a Lovely Place }

He's built quite a lovely place, really, in the woods out by Little Snoring, has Henry Howard, and indeed his wife Frances de Vere's there at this very moment, clipping the paws of her Shiatsus and having her eyelashes tinctured, and saying, "Voici, voilà, voici, voilà..." How sweet, they met in Chambercy fifteen years ago, this is the fifteenth anniversary of the day they met, they met over a glass of wine, their eyes met over a glass of her father's Pernand-Verglesses that had tumbled to a stone floor, they met at twilight! Well. She's finished with the dogs and there's some challenging needlepoint or for that matter she can have a glass of Pernand-Verglesses or else she can have one of the stable boys, Ardenzio, Trufaldino, or one of the older stable boys (older, but still boys), in the stable, and it will all be quite lovely, très gentil, très mignon, but alas up in London the Lady Columbine, who silently delivers his mail on a golden plate, has just brought Henry Howard notification that his head will be lopped off with a blunt axe and held up with the eyes still popping to get a rise out of a nauseating crowd half bored to death, on the 21st inst.; and that afterward, very soon afterward, soldiers of the King will come out to the woods near Little Snoring and tear down this beautiful estate. Tear down this beautiful estate, raze it to the ground, burn the beams to ashes, send the stable boys packing. It's really quite a beautiful setting for an estate, in a woods of towering aspen trees near a field of high soft blue grass where pink cows sleep. I've seen the place. And the stable boys are in the straw, writhing alone.

{ Red Ribbons }

I don't have anything to do with this, with any of this, except that I pick up the dossiers (all tied with red ribbon) and place them in correct order, and whispering my verses I sweep out the stalls of the official asses and official bulls, and I clean under the official desks, and I occasionally refill the pencil pots with freshly sharpened pencils. When something informative is set before me what licence do I have to disregard it? I put it to you.

{ Henry or Henry }

The Archbishop of Canterbury, Thomas Cranmer, is picking his nose. It's tea time, there are platters of cakes and ales and tea in great casks. He's got quite an audience— Pantalone the metaphysician who's hooked on the game called "Reduction," wherein he enunciates essential qualities ("Grape hyacinth: blueness, longitude, perspicacity, delicacy, rotundness"; "Flagon: portliness, promise, salutation"; and so on); that old codger Pianissimo, who plays the game called "Fingertip," finding as many places as possible to insert his fingertip; the moping cleric Nasturtio, playing "Ring-a-ding-ding," a game in which whenever a lady changes her composure upon a sofa he shakes a little bell, "Ring-a-ding-ding, ding-ding!"; the deaf mapmaker Flavio, playing "Nonce," a game in which he throws himself at the feet of any boy in pink; and many more. Someone, could it be shy and retiring Pierrot, says, "Do favor us with an opinion, Your Grace, about the horrible and pressing case of our dear King Henry VIII and our beloved Henry Howard, the Earl of Surrey; because the former has had my very dear friend Harlequin arrested for jesting in service of the latter, and the latter, it is true, has written verses capable of tickling the belly hairs of the Venus de Milo!" Touching his lips with his doily the Archbishop coyly replies, "Well, yes, well, yes, I predict it will be a case of Henry or Henry."

{ How is a Dogge lyk a Man? }

But what's the complot? Rich enough. Henry Howard Earl of Surrey gets a few last (perfunctory) jokes from his illegal jester Arlecchino, alias Harlequin (all spruced up in pink silks with yellow and black diamonds, and with his face half a smile and half a frown, and with his jiggle-stick drooping) and dies just after noon on the appointed day, hardly as yet a man. Howard's last words to Harlequin:

With all good fay I now before you stande
As destitute as any in ye lande
Unto ye dethe. My cyng must justly knowe
My faults do festere, and my wronge doth growe.
Farewell O fool, farewell this ertheliche clime
May naught deny you paradis or time
To souke fine nectars of ye wise man's roode
And turn yourself for claspyng but ye goodde.
A darke bitraisyng mars my way to pes
I wot not how to singe without this sadnesse
If e'er a Perseus chased a finer fles
Than I have lost with bold sorfete of gladnesse
I wot not. But holde: ye ax will droppe to cres
My gentler spirit with a strok of madnesse.

The Fool's last words to Howard:

How is a dogge lyk a man?
—Where'er he goes a tale followes him.

Then there are four more executions, a thief boy named
Braymer, the Dukes of Leicestershire and Norberly, sob-
bing and staining their pants, and the wife of Timothy Baron
of Argot whose tiaras are rudely confiscated by the Lord
Sheriff before she bares her neck. The coffins are piled high.
The fifth in line is Thomas Duke of Norfolk, Surrey's father, but even as the headsman has wiped his hands to raise
the axe for him lo, a cornet is sounded from the sunshot

parapets and the privy secretary to the Chamberlain, entering by way of a tiny door into the little courtyard which houses the scaffold, rather magisterially (and oddly without tears) makes the pronouncement, "The King is dead, long live the King." Immediately Harlequin to Amaril, aside: "Verily! Witness, boy, the perils of the sheets. Make bold, young man, to wipe your knife whenever you have used it to sliver your beef." Amaril to Harlequin: "I say, wot, sliver my beef!" Harlequin: "And what a black weight, sob, is the demise, sob, of Henry Howard, sob, a man whose poems have begun to sit sweetly with me, I admit. He always made his water on the hollyhocks, you know. But I pray his blank verse will ne'er be forgotten." Amaril: "Pfft! Fear not. It will surely be forgotten."

{ Great People }

The King is buried with great pomp, as befits great people. The royall bodye is carried in halting steps through the King's Garden, where there are two dozen posts bearing lions and unicorns all painted white and green; and paperwhite daffodils planted by Wolsey, whose ghost seems in the waving shrubbery to moan. Ye corpis is reported by several to be strongly malodorous and the region of the royall manlinesse quite without pareil. The squinting eyes of the lords and ladies attendant at the grave twist here and there to read the squinting eyes of the lords and ladies attendant at the grave. The King's dogs yelp inconsolably.

The King's last words, reported by Pandolfo by way of Pantalone by way of the Countess of Frangipane: "More mutton!"

{ Pity }

Pierrot, totally uninformed cloudface, thinks the King is in his bedchamber still a-thrashing upon Anne Boleyn, thinks the King is yet a boy…. (But Pierrot thinks the moon is made of cream.) And he is still in painful duteousness seeking poor Henry Howard, "Where is Sir Henry Howard?," for a counting of those elusive chinwhiskers. "I call, I call, I call upon the Earl of Surrey, oyez, oyez." Somebody—is it one of the stable boys, Ardenzio or Trufaldino?—takes pity on the dolt and brings the severed questioning head upon a plank.

{ Ye Lyrick of Historie }

An ending, did you say? Ardenzio and Trufaldino, those indomitable stable boys, having done with their sweaty work in the stables, their pleasant perspirations; and growing older; done with their richly fetid labors; now accreting years and years, marrying and having children, their children marrying and having children, and also the children's children making children, yes, through five coronations, through Edward VI and Jane Grey the nine days' Queen, and Mary and Elizabeth and James, so that it is newly be-

64

come the year 1613, a good enough time to go to the theatre: we take ourselves to the Globe (a place that really smells, half pissoir and half porringer) where what should be playing—indomitable coincidence!—but William Shakespeare's *The Life of King Henry VIII*. Scads of iambic pentameter: di-DA di-DA di-DA di-DA di-DA, as though history were but a song. And the obscure mazes of courtish intrigue all played again, but lyrically! And, lyrically, ye scafolde! Ye Lyrick of Historie. Someone at last: Cranmer, that lisping academic: is spitting out quite in the breath before ye finall courteyn,

> Ye birde of wundor dyes, ye Mayden Phoenix,
> Her Ashes newe create another Heyre,
> As grete in admiration as her Selfe;
> So shall she leve her blessednesse to one,
> Whenne heven shall calle her from this cloude of
>   darknes,
> Who from ye sacred Ashes of her Honor
> Shall Star-like rise, as greate in fame as she was,
> And so stande fix'd: pes, plenty, love, treuthe, teror—

when O!, there's a scream from the audience, a screme!, a screme!, and a second and a third, an explosion of screams, a fiery sea, culture of curses, calls on every side to God, O flames, fleyms, O pillars, pilars of fleym, bodies dropping and clawing, cleving, staumpyng, ye wayste congregation, ye poore harveste; and now, and enow, stage, play, moment, everything: up in smoke.

Imbroglio

EMACIATED epicene Imbroglio with a monstrous knife is carving a champignon. He's nipped away the base of the stem and slipped off the filthy prepuce and sly Ardenzio, who's taught him a thing or two about fluting, is watching him attempt to flute. It's far too big a blade—the blade's as big as a goose breast—and, truth is, he didn't learn a thing from that thyroid case Ardenzio so the little mushroom, adorable button, is flying pathetically into slivers in a thousand directions while off in the distance some hag tries her lungs at Giuseppi Veronaldi's "Mi credenza di peltazzo per dolor." What a miserable excuse for a song to begin with, and she's flaying it alive. It hasn't rained in weeks and weeks, the Princess of Zulpetsa's daisy beds have been given up for lost. Imbroglio is now being informed by Docteur Bruneto, very politely and succinctly if presumptuously, that there is no possibility he will graduate and become a maestro in the palatial kitchens of Landino. Morsels of mushroom, pinking, all over the straw-littered floor, with the three regimental piglets creeping around and sucking them up for snacks.

Let's get out there across the cheery courtyard (where the flagon wagon has gone almost off-balance upon the doltish curbstone, and two pallid musketeers are vying with tarot cards for the chance to climb the vines outside a young boy's window, and a scraggly wench is separating rotting from healthy golden peppers on an oily board, and a squire is drooling to polish a breastplate) to the dank and rancid chamber, perfumed by smouldering stagger-wort, where Eglantine the daughter of Tartaglia (Emissary of the Doge) is throwing her swollen lungs against that hallmark of contemporary culture, Giuseppi Veronaldi's "Mi credenza di peltazzo per dolor." There's her agonized maidservant, Filesia, lacing back the curtains to reveal blisters of vapid moonlight. So nice if for ten minutes it would rain and leave a mist. So nice if the singer could sing, but she couldn't save her life with a c-sharp. Magic if we could be persuaded to listen with all our hearts to an innuendo of lyrics but instead she's giving us heartburn by scrounging half of them from the abysmal love letters of Valerio Stupenzo to the Contessa di Frangipane; documents which have more or less tumbled into her hands (along with frilled panties), stuffed by mistake into a shipment of laundry from the steaming vats of Isabella di Laminafra (: huge oaken vats filled with tepid water in which plump hypersensitive girls with their skirts strapped up by snakeskins and with orchidaceous bandanas cupped over their coily hair step rhythmically and with a delirious rotation of the hips, making bubbles that smell somewhat of lamb.) But that song, that abysm: "You, you, of my dreams...you, you, of my reverie…whose breasts, whose breasts, are figs and walnuts…whose breasts delight my lips, my lips, my scarred tongue…" It's queer about Eglantine the daughter of Tartaglia (Emissary of the Doge) seeming a hag, because it's true that all the time she was growing up everybody said of her if only she'd keep her mouth shut her beauty would exceed tangerines. Something about the discoloration of her teeth, from eating pound after pound of that infamous cheese from Abruzzi and chocolate from Torrento and cold pickled eel from Castellammare. Delectation of furtive, slithering moonlight, yet where is a bowl of goat's milk, polluted Ofanto water, anything to wet the tonsils? And speaking of tonsils, that song again, that incalculable "Mi credenza di peltazzo per dolor," a melody which would bring tears of sympathy from the moonlit statue of Giuseppi Veronaldi who wrote it if only the three giddy adolescents, Porenzo, Lorenzo and Credenzo weren't busy urinating in unison up and down its legs.

The unhappy engagement of Valerio Stupenzo to the Contessa di Frangipane ensues: It has to do with a miserable fig tree. The fig tree in question grows in the Contessa's yard. The keeper of the yard is one-eyed Smagegga, who has been teaching himself over these anxious years to converse with doves. "Oooo, cooo, loooo," yes. And there is much in conversation with doves that you do with fingers. But the Contessa's enormous corpulence, a sign of great worthiness in her large family, is maintained by a diet of figs. And on his side, Valerio Stupenzo's ailing father must have figs to keep him from dying, so proclaims Docteur Bruneto making notes in a garbled script and producing a chain of framboise-flavored hiccups. Young Valerio creeps at night over the rough-rock wall until he is in the silent, fragrant garden with the Contessa di Frangipane's fig tree. And there: Smagegga, picking her nightly portion with a dove upon each shoulder. Whereupon Valerio Stupenzo comes out of the shadows and says, "Estimable Smagegga, keeper of the Contessa's figs, confidant of birds, pray let me have a small basket to take to my ailing father, Don Horacio Stupenzo, who will cause the figs to be slit and roasted almonds to be inserted in their crevices before popping them into his mouth, just as the wise Docteur Bruneto has ordered." But for some reason Smagegga is moved, instead of handing over figs, to play the provocative but distracting game, "Undo!," as follows: every time Valerio Stupenzo reaches out for a fig from his basket Smagegga leans forward, unties one of the fine little knots that is fastening Valerio's purple silk jerkin, and wails, "Undooo!" The doves, of course, think he's talking to them and start ooooing madly. Tying himself up again, Valerio pleads, "Oh, kind Smagegga, do permit me a fig to give my ailing father, for in months it has not rained and in the heart of the fig is the moisture of the gods, so announces the wise Docteur Bruneto," and again the groundskeeper unfastens the jerkin, "Undoooo!" Then: "Sweet Smagegga, oh conscientious Smagegga, grant me the boon of a pair of figs, as the wise

Docteur Bruneto advises," and the jerkin comes undone again, "Undoooooo!" "Permit me a fig!," the jerkin is almost removed, "Undooooooooo!" "Cede me a fig," three knots are undone, "Undoooooooooooooooo!" "—because the all-knowing, all-curing Docteur Bruneto—" And the doves are bending over trying to make themselves understood, "Vooo, cooo, loooo, stoooo, chooooooo." Now Smagegga, having thoroughly stripped the prince, whispers in a Romagnese dialect, "Come, I'll show you *my* fig for a penny or twooooo!"

Valerio decides to abandon this activity and commit himself to the safety of quill and parchment.

> My dearest Contessa di Frangipane, would it be opportune, would it be conceivable, might it be thinkable that you would allow, that you might entertain the possibility of, that you might be persuaded to countenance the notion that

But who is this importunate beggar! Tearing his note to shreds before with bulbous eyes she can have swallowed its purport she commands that the writer be delivered before her, his elbows handicapped with thin bracelets of leathery sausage, his neck weighted with a trio of upside-down plucked guinea fowl. She is dreaming of delicious punishments, biting out the hairs of his chest one by one.... But on seeing Valerio Stupenzo she falls passionately in love: he is youth, he is light, he is movement! Make the fig tree over to him in writing she will, she promises, and in front of the great judge Scaramouche to boot, if only he, upon a full moon, will mount her in the wet grass by the swan pond, and thence, not to tarry but to marry, lest she parry.... Poor innocent Valerio Stupenzo, this woman is so obese a specimen even her eyelashes are daunting—in summer, he has heard, like strands of twine they stiffen when her salty perspiration dries and hordes of weary insects perch upon them to sleep.

So the kid sells off his innocence (or his callowness; it's one or the other), dropping his pretense, his purple jerkin (and much else) for a plateful of figs, a basketful of succulent figs, to drop upon the bed of his ailing father. Don Horacio eats so ravenously he is soon transformed into a staunch knight radiating color and robustness and good looks, *Prestodigitato!* Exactly the sort of subject most adored by such as the great limner Mezzetinto.... (Docteur Bruneto, meanwhile, freed from diagnosing him, plays the game of "Frog," mounting every lady he can find in a punctilious squat and, yes, attempting with his bluish tongue to captivate flies.) Don Horacio Stupenzo, galloping through hill and dale on his trusty steed, crying out (and why?, no one has a clue), "O for England, for England!"....

Mezzetinto is gravely at a loss trying to limn a portrait of that staunch knight radiating color and robustness and good looks, and crying out, "O for England, for England!," Don Horacio Stupenzo. In what wise? For openers, he is accustomed to the inspiration of the sallow Princess of Zulpetsa darning tapestries by his side as he limns, because she will frequently look up—it is her custom frequently to look up—and exclaim, "How stimulating!" over his shoulder. A kind of optic aphrodisiac, since staring at his handiwork he is led to imagine the fulness of her suppurations. But this morning, woe, the Princess of Zulpetsa's daisy beds having been given up for lost in the continuing drought, she has been condemned to forego her post-prandial game of "He Loves My Left Breast, He Loves My Right" (an exercise for the spinal column, conducted with the aid of the petals of one of those gigantic flowers), and has employed the groom Pulcinello instead to assist her manually. The groom possesses enormous, but very delicate, fingers. "I love your left breast. I love your right. I love your left breast. I love your right." So that she cannot bring herself to get recorseted until long after the sun has reached mid-sky, bringing on that hazy torpor which leads all sensible beings to insert themselves between sheets.

The painter's difficulty, however, is worsened. There is the problem of perspective, under the best of circumstances a taxing conundrum. Everyone has gathered round to play

the game called "Look From Here." (1) Don Horacio
Stupenzo is on a platform, seated upon a barrel of olives
covered with red and purple Chinese brocade. He has one
fat leg crossed over the other. People are viewing him. (2)
Scaramouche has gone off behind a pear tree and is peeping
through a knothole: "Mezzetinto, look from here!" (3)
Filesia is lying on her back staring up Don Horacio's skirt
to see if she can tell whether his hose are fastened with or
without a cord: "Mezzetinto, it's wonderful if you look from
here!" (4) Imbroglio and Ardenzio are hanging from the
boughs of a weeping willow, and, because for months it has
not rained, the leaves are dry and shuffle hysterically as the
two struggle to scratch their bums. They think this aerial
view is magnificent: "Mezzetinto, from here, from here, you
have to see it from here!" (5) The Princess of Zulpetsa has
arrived finally and contrives to swirl in great arabesques
around the little platform where Don Horacio is perched,
seeing him always in great swoops of melodious undula-
tion: "From here, Mezzetinto, from here!" (6) Eglantine
the daughter of Tartaglia (Emissary of the Doge) still keeps
at that hideous song, so her eyes are closed. (7) Porenzo,
Lorenzo and Credenzo have dug a pit, "From heeeeere!,"
and (8) Isabella di Laminafra the public launderess is catch-
ing Don Horacio's dignified silhouette cast with the help of
the blazing sun through the Contessa di Frangipane's newly-
starched pillowcases which she is suspending from a creeper
vine. Even if Mezzetinto could pick an ideal point of vantage, however, he'd never be prepared for what comes next.
That barrel of olives Don Horacio is ensconced upon has

traveled for eleven months with the drought, beginning in Seville and proceeding by way of Abu-Bakkad-el-Bakkad quite as far as the Golfo di Manfredonia, so that this afternoon, under the Don's capacious pressure, it simply gives up the ghost. With a munificent slap the boards disintegrate into a thousand useless fragments and the great man collapses in a heap upon Filesia's face. Brine everywhere. Lizard-green olives are forming patterns in the dirt, constellations, arcane symbols, the symbol of the wounded boar.... Somebody hears Mezzetinto muttering hopelessly to himself, "Bring on the Quattrocento! It can't come soon enough to give us a way out!"

Don Horacio Stupenzo has been asked to squat on a rock and the painting has again begun. But the third and consummate problem is that because for weeks there has been no rain Mezzetinto the master limner can do nothing about his colors. Not a color can be mixt without arabic water, surely, Gume Arrabecke Watter throwne togethyr from the watters of the reservoire into whych the reynes doe falle. Normally it is his practice to utilize a palate both complicated and rich:

Quicksiluer (Quicksilver white)
Veluet blacke (Velvet black)
Charkecole blacke (Charcoal black)
Willowecolle (Willowcoal black)

Peach black, from the stones of peches

Blacke sugarcandye (Black sugar lake)

Oyle of whit popy (White poppy)

Whitlead (White lead)

Serusa (Fine ceruse white)

Cornation (Carnation white)

Ossium white, made from the burnt bones of a pig still
young (or the bones of a Lambe, and of yong burnt,
also of some sheels, as ege sheels)

Chery black, from chery stones (cherry stones)

Venice lake

Antwerpen murreye (Antwerp murrey, which is not as
good as Venice lake, except for peacocks)

India stammel (a red)

Vermelion (Vermilion)

Venice ultramarine

Litmouse blewe (Litmus blue)

Indy blewe (Indigo blue)

Verditer

Massicot

Dull massicot, which be a mixture of massicot and pink,
good for cheeks

Pauncy greene (pansy-green)

Masticott yeallowe (Massicot yellow)

Oker (ochre)

Oxe gall yeallowe (Yellow gall, which be of gall stones ground,
but not fishes' gall)

earth of cullen (Earth brown of Köln)

ochre de rouse

> Not to mention the stones, rubye and annatist and
> saphier and emarod and topias orientall

Now he has been able to prepare nothing, noe watter, noe
reyne, but he can draw only on a volume of the cherry black,
from cherry stones, because the Contessa di Frangipane has
caused a cartload of cherries to be dragged from her estates
in Squinzano by those two hearties, Ubaldo and Gesualdo,
who fear flogging. Fere of flaugynge. The cherry black is a
rich one, moistened with pressure of cherries, but it is the
only color he has, so the entire portrait must be black, cherry
black, a delicious thing to behold and yet impossible to dis-
cern. "I am a futurist," says Mezzetinto, painting the black
moustache over the black lips upon the black face, and in
the distance touching up a black turret upon a cherry black
castle upon a cherry black hill. Hearing the word "Futurist" somebody—Imbroglio?—slips in and feeds him the idea
of a meal: ziti with poached eggs, pumpkin, boiled liver,
peaches and asparagus.

But meanwhile the game of "Asparagus" is being carried
forth by Ubaldo and Gesualdo. They've hoarded some very
plump stalks of asparagus, also from the estates in
Squinzano, and over the many weeks, the many many
weeks, of traveling and hoarding, the stalks have softened
and gone profoundly limp. Now the trick is to hold your
flaccid asparagus by the base and engage your friend in a

spirited duel, as though the asparagus were swords of Venus, yes, drooping utensils. The local women, Lady Flaminia, the effervescent Franceschina, lofty Isabella, lovely Lidia, stand around captivated in whispers and throaty giggles as, *thwack thwack*, the muted pendulous asparaguses slap against one another at slapdash angles and finally in a frenzy of dedication Ubaldo's is snapped in half. "Reward for your virtue!" cries lovely Lidia, and flings herself into Gesualdo's arms at precisely the best angle for devouring the man's lengthy vegetable in a single slurping bite. [Some students later regarded this ritual as a fertility ceremony and gave it a highly ramified symbology. See Thurgood and Tensen, 1881; Orpington, 1908; Auck, 1923; Richards and Cumberly, 1939; and Craype, 1988.]

Lady Flaminia has cut every excess rose to leave a perfect ring of roses in the Conservatory (especially designed as a cloistered garden with a springing fountain—from which you cannot drink—surrounded by a ring of roses) and now she is arranging her freshly cut roses in Imbroglio's pantry in a crystal goblet. The morning sunlight is dripping down on her, a slight breeze is rippling the tamarisk fronds just outside the window, she's got some golden clippers and has carefully selected the roses one by one and snipped their bases for length and pounded their new-cut bases with the handles of the golden clippers. Here and there she boldly fights off a low-springing leaf. Rose colors: There are pallid pink roses like corals, and those darkening by shades of pink until they are as deep as a cloud of sunset suspended in a cathedral between the yawning panes of the cathedral's colored glass. Now the morning sunlight is covering Lady Flaminia with her roses. She has made the paler roses shorter, the darker roses taller toward the center. And she's moving on to an arrangement of pink carnations and lavender tulips, it's pathetic with the pendulous thick green leaves of the tulips cascading over the lip of the vase. Harlequin is observing. Secretly. Nothing on earth gives him more pleasure than - - - - to watch Lady Flaminia - - - - arranging - - - - flowers - - - - shhhhh. The attar of the roses floats over him. Thinks Harlequin caught in fascination for the roses, "Now time has stopped."

Harlequin and Scaramouche are doing a quadrille to pray for rain. The first, clothed in his puffy cloak of many-colored diamonds, raises his right leg and left arm and cries out, "Yaga polenta! Lapika lapuka!" Then his left leg and right arm: "Tchi, tchai, tchou!" And then, whirling his brittle three-cornered hat each arrogant prong of which is sharp enough to be a stiletto, the other bellows from the vibrant cavern of his entrails, "Hoagh! Foukh!" They move. They move in what begins as a circle and ends as a parallelogram. Black clouds coagulate in the western sky. There is the sound of thunder,

Koom!
Kombaraloom!
Kooma anda dooma!

Filesia and Don Horacio Stupenzo are licking the olive brine
from one another's shoulders, whispering, "Pickle! Pickle!"
Magnesium lightning sends shudders across Scaramouche's
shoulder blades and relieves the descending throes of his
lumbago. Nearby, in the cloistered garden with the springing fountain from which you cannot drink and the ring of
pink roses, Eglantine the daughter of Tartaglia (Emissary
of the Doge) is still squeezing her vocal cords through the
impossible apertures of Giuseppi Veronaldi's "Mi credenza
di peltazzo per dolor." May the rain fall upon her in boat-
loads! In all sincerity I must protest that the sound of her
voice is an excruciation to gentled ears. She is become a
veritable Iron Maiden in the torture chamber of civilization. And because of the catastrophic sound of her, does
not each man weep in the singular knowledge that his days
and the days of his friends will forever be known with contempt as The Dark Ages?

On the vast parterres are great semicircles of horehound,
now in the rains become intoxicating again. Imbroglio the
assistant chef lies there, the membranes of pounds of mushrooms scattered across his chest. Ravenous for mushrooms
after all his mushroom fluting he has devoured all the mush-

rooms that were fluted. Having sated himself on mushrooms he has the hunger for fiction, ye hongre for fyxionne. He proceeds in the obvious way to dream the lost legends of Araby.

Somehow in the great thunderstorm, so bombastic the magnolia blossoms have all shuddered into the river, the many-colored balloon bouquets of the Comtesse di Frangipane have gone all airless, quite pathetic, so that now hanging from the lofty boughs of her trysting tree are only so many vivid bladders unable to stop themselves from flopping this way and that according to the merest chances of the breeze. "Any one of those could be me," says a voice from behind a bush, but as soon as we chase it down, parting the thorns from before our cheeks, we discover that there is no one there.

Porenzo, Lorenzo and Credenzo are having a little discussion about the pleasure of the mouth, while behind them on a long table raisins marinated in gentian, safflower oil and rosemary are stuffed into the nostrils of a boar. "How nature manifests itself in everything cooked!" sings Credenzo, "How the smells of the earth rise up from every morsel on the table! Why, that boar once roamed the paleolithic forests of Smagny-Laboisse, and scraps of the very truffles buried there in blackest loam even now do gleam from the putrid cleavages of its feet!" Lorenzo is more pragmatic: "I imagine to myself what it will taste like, when it has been basted a dozen times in shallot butter and baked in a lake of Paulliac and cream. I imagine a glass of Champagne, and a little dish of roasted potatoes." Porenzo, however: "I can only say, how philosophically pregnant is the insertion into those critical organs of olfaction, of objects sacrificed to the all-illuminating beams of the life-giving sun. This animal, round and perfect, will surely symbolize intelligence, civilization, conscience, aspiration, truth,…and I myself will be especially attentive to every delicate possibility of thought and understanding when like a barbarian I hurl myself into the act of tearing its flesh between my well-ordered teeth."

Columbine and Pierrot have been on a hilltop, beautiful hilltop, overlooking all of this amazing scenario: nothing have they failed to see or hear. "What do you think? What do you think," says Pierrot tapping Columbine on the elbow, "What do you suppose? What do you suppose?" She gives a little smile. Now, "There could still be just a little more," says she with a twinkle in her blue blue eye, and reaching into the crazy realm with a cautious hand she deposits a mouse.

Sicilian Vespers

THE THIRTEENTH of July, 1789, twilight. Weary of the way people breeze past him in the streets without tipping their hats respectfully, Corviello the mushroom-king decides it's time to call a general Characters' meeting ostensibly for the purpose of electing a suitable consort for Scaramouche (but really to attract a little attention as a doer of remarkable deeds) before the artisans throw open the Bastille (as it's rumored they will first thing in the morning changing all of history and incidentally making it impossible for at least eleven years to hear yourself think). Listen, one can't have seen anyone uglier, smarmier, more contemptible, more unapproachable, on the face of this earth, than the invidious Scaramouche, to whom we finally consider it appropriate, if not merely convenient, to deliver some measure of happiness. But why, alors, since long it's been well-known his blandishments are more tortuous than Marie Antoinette's?

Because he's pathetic. He's got his salon hung floor-to-ceiling, for starters, with Bouchers: yes, splayed thighs, apricot crevices, of women with the faces of infants open promises in every direction. But where's the real thing, heh? I'll tell you where, nowhere. The serving maidens rush around dusting the furniture as though it's a hundred-meter dash, not surprising since he's got the speediest fingers this side of Vincennes. Dignified creatures, children of noble birth, wouldn't be caught dead in his precincts, won't stop for camomile tea even if he does have lemon cakes imported from Geneva to go along with it, can't speak his name at the Palais-Royal without blushing incontrovertibly and losing control of their digestion. What is it about him, that habit of massaging stallion sweat (direct from the Bois) into his biceps? Or can it be his nasty predilection for words beginning with "u"? Or the fact that although his embroidered dress coats (of mauve, of greenish-pink, of silvery-blue taffeta) most alluringly plead to the eye, nevertheless his breeches (invariably of gold silk) fit somewhat too bravely where he's wont to sit, and his red hose have runs produced as he scratches his itchy legs with dirty untrimmed fingernails? What an excuse for a man! And his behavior is legendary, he has not a kind word for anyone, curses like malodorous suspirations swim away from his thick lips, his connexions to the police are well-documented…But wait; Scaramouche, beneath all this, is the figure of a man obsessed by love. And why should it not be true? His frail heart pounds when a certain lady passes by, his eyes flood o'er with tears, his hands go limp and wet, his many thousands of bank accounts dwindle away to mist. And worse—

He develops a passionate craving for mushrooms. To sate which he makes his way to the private apartments of Corviello and, baring his soul, dines on seventeen varieties until the small hours, with Puligny-Montrachet and fresh soft buttered bread. Here the servants are not unaccustomed to playing a naughty game on him, "Investments," in which they make him sign pieces of paper before laying the delicacies before him one at a time. One piece of paper for each mushroom—and he signs and he signs. Some of the pieces of paper have writing upon them already. He does not notice. He breathes quickly. His passion for mushrooms is inconsummable. His neck reddens. His wrists twitch. He signs more and more furiously, and the great fat mushrooms are laid before him, one after another, on gold-edged plates. He licks them. He gnaws at the tender rills on the underside of the caps. Sweat breaks out on his cheeks, his eyes close. He signs pages with his eyes shut. His breathing rises in pitch, as though climbing a ladder to heaven. He signs pages he can barely detect and the dark ink smears and stains his hand. Suddenly, with a huge moan, he collapses upon his plates, a mushroom half-eaten in his trout-white palm.

The town hall isn't half big enough to hold the crowd Corviello's marshalled, given the unfortunate fact that Mezzetinto and his fourteen morons have got their scaffolding spangled as far as the eye can see for the purpose of cleaning up the frescoes da Vinci's brother-in-law's cousin's wife's former boyfriend Smagegga put down. Horrible pictures of cupids holding grapes. Big clamor to gather outside next to the open well, which is fetid, for the game called "Cosmetics" and the audience in the parterres goes crazy when fat Scaramouche is strapped into a chair and then hoisted onto a platform to be perfumed in public with *fond de pissenlit* (in the revered tradition). "I adore you, I adore you all," bellows he in a voice filled with loathing as they're yellowing his loose skin, "I worship the freckles on your children's sunny little faces." Fearsome. They're annointing him now with sprigs of brittle sumac and oil extracted from rancid eggplants and somebody tickles underneath his arm with a half-cooked eel. Somebody else (it may well have been Cassandro himself) walks around the fat man in ever-widening circles blowing farts. And now it's been decided, Yes, the perfect plump happy wife would be Blanchette, who sits at the feet of old Docteur Polichinelle polishing his briefcases, except that the other women have reasons of their own for wanting an alignment—"I adore every last one of you. I will release you for life from the obligation of having to pay your taxes"—so that as Cassandro lowers the pitch of his farts they step forward and (to twirping balalaika music) play the awkward game, "Fruit Bowl," in which it's necessary to guess whether to treat the great lord Scaramouche as a kumquat, or a tangerine, or a damson plum, or just as a banana.

And the winner is Smeraldine, deaf since earliest childhood. "Hoohah," is all she can say, with timidest breath, and her eyes roll upward, her forest green eyes, and her fingers carve the air in miraculous palpitation. "Hoohah."

But before the marriage Scaramouche gets the Inhibitions, a curious malady symptomatized by frozen smiles and stains on the nether-garments. Clearly a speech must be made by the imperious Docteur Bruneto, who's arrived with his brother-in-law, the limping poet Sforzetto. The imperious Docteur Bruneto has little to recommend but extracts of verbena and toadwort for smoothing the wrinkles of wedding nights. This leads the crowd into the entertainment called "Toadwort," in which Scaramouche's every utterance is loudly interrupted, *"Toadwort!"* "I'm very happy, Docteur, that you could come, because—" *"Toadwort!"* "Marriage will definitely suit me, because I'm so—" *"Toadwort!"* "I have truly never felt better in my—" *"Toadwort!"* And so on. Here, however, Sforzetto breaks into a spontaneous paean to the hardiness and tribulations of the marvelous Marie Antoinette, who's had nothing but adventures, it turns out, at her many childbirths:

> Well, my dears, it was December, 1778, the 11th day of the month, and, *mon Dieu!*, what a bitch winter we'd been having, in case you've forgotten. The dear sweet Queen finally began feeling her pains at around

tea-time. Everybody who was anybody passed the night in the rooms adjoining the Queen's bedchamber but nothing—nothing, and then nothing again for more than a week. *Mon Dieu!* She kept it until the 19th, *mon Dieu!* Well, and then poor Marie was almost smothered! The etiquette of allowing absolutely anyone to come in at the moment of a Queen's delivery was observed so rigidly, *mon Dieu!*, that at the moment when Vermond, the *accoucheur*, cried out, *Elle va s'accoucher, la Reine!* the piles of inquisitive beings, *mon Dieu!*, who poured into the bedchamber made such a tumult, *mon Dieu!*, that the rush nearly destroyed the Queen. You couldn't move anywhere there was such a motley crowd! *Mon Dieu*, I thought I was in a gaming room on the Rue Cascard!

But that's hardly all. *Mon Dieu*, no! Her second pregnancy was a nightmare. It was the 22nd of October, 1781, I remember because dear Meublier had given six of us a surprise party with cakes from Salpeux's. I went to have a look—it must have been three o'clock in the morning! A silence like death was in the room, *mon Dieu!*, and at the instant the child came out the Queen truly thought she had only produced a daughter! But then the King went up to the bed and said to her, "Madame, you have fulfilled my wishes, and those of France; you are the mother of a dauphin." *Mon Dieu!*, let me tell you, that let the cat out of the bag!

Sforzetto's a wispy fragment of a man whose eyes rotate like weathervanes and he's bursting now with the curious assertion that to fix everything gargantuan Scaramouche need only regale the audience with a song. In this, it must be admitted, he shows no lack of responsibility to his poetic nature:

> Sing, sing, sing, Scaramouche, or
> I'll slit my own throat with a razor.
> I'll slit it, I'll split it
> I hereby admit it,
> So sing!

"*Sssssssing!*" roars Scaramouche, "Nothing of the sort!" "Oh, so then you *won't*? Well, if you *won't* sing, I'll *not* cut my throat either":

> Sing, sing, sing, infidel, or
> I'll thrust myself into a fire,
> I'll thrust myself, bust myself,
> Quite readjust myself,
> Sing!

Scaramouche's dignity is offended now, because even though it's true he craves profoundly to sing he never could learn how to drop his voice a perfect third: "Not a chance." "Ah, then if you *won't* sing, I'll *not* thrust myself either. Poof, basta!—"

Sing, sing, sing, Scaramouche
And I'll drink, and I'll drink belladonna,
I'll drink that pink stink
I'll shrink and I'll blink,
So sing!

Mortified with embarrassment, Scaramouche twitters, "No, no, no! No singing, no ringing, no bringing of relief from me to you." Whereupon Sforzetto is irremediably offended and cries, "You *won't* sing, so I certainly *won't* drink that offensive liquid, and may *that* give you pleasure on your wedding night." This is the revelry called "Not You, Not Me." (An interesting incidentalism: Years ago, the Comtesse di Frangipane had been engaged to provide cunning Scaramouche with voice lessons but had unutterably failed [arthritis blocked her fingers at the dulcimer], consequently today the life of the noble poet Sforzetto has been spared, *thrice!* More than once before this has happened, or Sforzetto'd certainly have had to slit his throat while the fat man mooned off-key at his command, and then who'd there be to captivate us with stories about the royal family?)

Having proceeded to his garret on the rue des Prêtres Saint Germain l'Auxerrois the poet's composing (in tiny meticulous glyphs strung out in a tiny leathered book) the ending of the masterpiece that will later be known as *The Pensive Child*:

"Who is it?" said the lady-in-waiting coldly.

"One who reads the catalogue of his faults by thy light," came the answer.

"But your faults are tinier than fleas."

"And your kindness in saying so is magnified, even though already it is overwhelming."

A sudden inspiration seized the stranger. "Surely you recognize that

when oops!, he's interrupted by a bell at his own door, and standing to answer it is overcome by a desire to taste freshly pickled gherkins. Already in a swaggering posture against the lintel, however, is Lelio the rake, fiddling disconsolately with his broad tricorne and moaning that the sumptuous Lady Flaminia has declined an opportunity to mother him: "Her breasts, in which I might bury myself! Her arms, in which I am drowning! Her loins, in which gratefully I would lose my passage! Indeed her fingertips, which control my dreaming as the tailfeathers of pigeons shape the wind!" And outside the audience is cheering stupidly because Scaramouche has actually brought himself to sing "Jolie Mariette avec ses vingt garçons" and also "Cu-cu-ri-cu Garimanzi" and also, but hopelessly out of key, "Al fato dan legge quegli occhi vezzosi" from *Così Fan Tutte* with half the words changed to la-la-la.

Deaf Smeraldine's cooking a soup in which she's put both peanuts and pasta, both tripe and truffles, both shrimp and sherry, both dolmadakia and dandelions, both broccoli and beluga caviar, both yams and yeast, both kippers and kvass, both nesselrode and neat's foot jelly, both rose hips and rice vinegar, both gruyère and green peppercorns. "Hoohah." She moves with delicious smallness, every motion with the golden ladel small, every opening and closing of the moist mouth small, every flicker of the toes small upon the bamboo mat floor. Think of it, her world is all silent. Except she can feel the Hhh of the air coming in and out of her, "Hoohah": otherwise all the world is gracious and delicate in its silent motion. Gracious in silent motion are the elements of the soup floating, both lamb shanks and lentils, both celery spikes and caramelized ginger…

Mezzetinto is watching her from the skylight, unbeknownst to fat Scaramouche who in an instant would despatch his mauve-clad myrmidons to slice the trembling artist into morsels. Mezzetinto has concocted an image-recording device, forerunner of what in thirty-five years Niépce (remembering da Vinci) will call his "petite chambre obscure," which is like a paper airplane and like a planter for holding geraniums and like a fish pond and like ten minutes in the presence of His Holiness Pope Pius VI. He's using it even now to image Smeraldine as slowly, delicately she moves, but the process is a slow process, hours upon hours are taken up by it, and he contents himself all the while by playing the game called "Who?" It's an easy game, you just ask questions about your environment, and it helps very nicely to pass the time, but you're nowhere near satisfied the further you go: "*Who* invented the soup she's cooking? *Who* carved her wooden spoon (with three goldfish)? *Who* set the window here on the rooftop (one of three windows)? *Who* named the three birds perched on the tree branch by my left shoulder? *Who* was the first person to make jam of lingonberries?" And so on. I could take the easy way out and say he falls asleep up there, playing that game. Some days it's true he does. Today, however, he doesn't fall asleep, he's startled instead by voices in the street below, and the voices are becoming tumultuous. It's turned out that because she nibbled his piece of the wedding cake Professeur Pantalon has thrown his wife of thirty years, Madame Leda, headfirst into the river. 14th of July, early in the morning.

They're fishing her out. It would be nice to think hundreds of folk have rushed over to help, but in truth everybody's occupied storming the Bastille, dragging that asshole the Marquis de Launay through the dirt and now ripping him to shreds. A man who was stupid enough to think they'd just stand there smiling if he put up a white flag, imagine, so they tapped their feet while he let the drawbridge down and, bango! They're running this way and that with the handful of prisoners and some lunatics and a couple of forgers and one grinning sadist on their shoulders. But back at the river, Old Cola's fishing Leda out from a barge. She's barely alive. Hesitantly, of all things, she's singing. Witnesses bend over to catch the lyrics. It's "Durch Zärtlichkeit und Schmeicheln" from *Die Entführung aus dem Serail*. The sun is covered swiftly by a cloud. Soldiers are pummeling some kids who've thieved two mackerel under one of the bridges. While the Lady Flaminia wraps her head in bandages sopping Leda begins to tell the story of her life. Professeur Pantalon, she says, is a good husband, everybody knows that, but he's gone out of his mind with anxiety, having misplaced his lecture notes on Mahmud of Ghazni. Crawling under the Lady Flaminia's skirts is gaunt Lelio, whimpering, sniffing, finally snoozing. And now it develops there's been another sort of tragedy, Corviello has borrowed the lecture notes of Professeur Pantalon for wiping off the knife he's been using to cut Scaramouche's six-tiered cake and all that's legible at this point is something obscure about child-labor in a sultanate near Delhi in August of 1027. Leda moves on to "Nie werd' ich Deine Huld verkennen" and somebody, not that cynical reprobate Tartaglia to be sure but one of his Slav neighbors over on the Quai de la Mégisserie, knocks against a cage and lets three ostrich hens loose. Now they've crossed over to the Left Bank, now they're bounding toward the Champ de Mars where Robespierre's holding a caucus, what a crazy world this is in which so many feathers can come loose because of only a wedding.

Contriving ways to catch glimpses of the Lady Flaminia as she disrobes by manipulating multiple mirrors with long twigs from nearby windows, Sforzetto and Lelio while away three and a half years. Finally Lelio succeeds, but she spies him spying. They play the game called "I See You Seeing Me Seeing You," in which minute examinations of hairy areas are undertaken and the germs of philosophies of introspection and self-referentiality develop. But things soon get unbearable—the Lady Flaminia's arrested as a confidante of the Queen, and Lelio with her as a confidante's confidant, and after a perfunctory trial the manner in which the democratic mob plans to put them to death is too hideous to describe (see, for circumlocution, Vaxeur de Bontesquieu, 1819, pp. 934–977).

Finally, twilight. The dogs are holding back their woofing on the black barges in the river. Stopping into Nôtre Dame—all candle-light orange upon the stones—for her nightly orations, the dimpled Columbine, distraught after a long day scattering flower petals into passing tumbrels, meets up with her importunate lover Arlequin. It would be crazy not to mention that she's a real pâtisserie. The mass is almost over, the voluminous silences are already echoing into the great blue-shadowed vaults. How many millions of unhappy people there are in this shuddering city, how many do not yet sleep, and there are the hundreds, she knows, whose heads will keep rolling sleepless every day. Indeed,

hasn't the sotted poet Sforzetto confided this particular tid-
bit to her?: "My dear, I've had it from the first lady of the
second bedchamber, so it can hardly be more reliable:

One evening, in May, the Queen was sitting in her
room, when somebody came in and lit four wax
candles upon her toilette. The first went out immediately, and I took the liberty of re-lighting it. Soon
enough the second went out as well. Then the third
was doused. At which point Her Majesty, squeezing
my hand in terror, said: 'Misfortune has the power to
make us superstitious; if the fourth taper goes out as
well I will surely interpret it as a fatal omen.' Whereupon the fourth taper blinked out.

No, my little innocent, it doesn't look good." But, "My love
for you," says Arlequin meanwhile, since one might as well
make one's proclamations, "is as endless as the sky. Believe
me, believe me, dear Columbine. If you do nothing else on
earth, pray believe me." She: "Whether I believe you or
not, Arlequin, surely I am yours as long as garlics shall
grow." Then he: "My love for you, Columbine, is much
richer than the earth. Believe me, believe me, my love is
richer than persimmons." She: "Whether I believe you or
do not believe you, I will go with you wherever you will
have me go. That your love is richer than persimmons I
may believe, or I may not believe, as I see fit." He: "It is true
that I have wanted you since the beginning of time, and

that I will want you in every country in every age. Believe me, dear Columbine, believe me." She: "I think that I do not believe you, Arlequin, but nevertheless it is true that you will never lose me." He: "I love you, then, as I love cognac, dear Columbine. I love you as I love Château de Mirambeau 1704." She: "I, too, love cognac, how curious! I love cognac more than swimming in the Grand Canal at Versailles when nobody's looking, and it is true Château de Mirambeau 1704 is not to be impeached. But it is also pleasant to lie on my back in a field of newmown barley with a picnic basket tucked between my legs." But instead of a barley field she lets him take her across the street to a bistro in the Lyonnais style and fill her with dinner (the fromage blanc comes in a big glass bowl), and after dinner she agrees to taste a bottle of Château de Mirambeau 1792. Glass after glass slips down that alabaster throat and it may as well be ancient it tastes so fine. "Arlequin," says Columbine, "If you will tell me again that you love me as endlessly as the earth, now I will believe you."

Onward the Revolution! Everybody's chattering that it's reminiscent of the Sicilian Vespers, nobility's head dropping like a tennis ball wherever you look, the beribboned hair and gilded vestments clipped and sold as souvenirs. The soup Smeraldine's simmered in her silence feeds not only piggish Scaramouche but many thousands of common mouths as well because we're all in it together. Now, and tomorrow, and throughout the revolution. The tax collector is devilish in his ways, throwing his victims mercilessly to the machine of the revolution, teeth of the machine of the revolution, dull teeth that chew slowly, but he surely profits, don't think for a moment nobody's up there profiting from the revolution and that everything's being shared out equally, because there are plenty of tyrants whose heads aren't falling salting goodies away carefully in the sinews of the new beast that's coming alive. No, the bells can ring and ring as they did in Sicily but Scaramouche never dies. The Scaramouches of our world don't ever die.

When night has fallen and the people have retired to their beds, disconsolate Pierrot emerges to tread the glistening alleyways. He's all in his whites, flaming up and then disappearing from puddles of lamplight. In the midst of catastrophe, beauty. First his gown shuffles to the left, then his gown shuffles to the right. It's only traces he's searching for in this darkness, traces of the affairs of men. Moonlight finally catches him in the vast reaches of the park of the Tuileries, underneath the great elms, he's like a white stag in the empty park pacing slowly from shadow to shadow. Do you want to really know him, this Pierrot? All of these creatures, these caricatures who fill our pages, are but dreams of his. He dreams to music, the tickle of the river against abutments, the parading shrill sigh of birds passing overhead on their way to the east. A day will finally come (he's fully aware) when he'll be noticed by nobody. After that, oblivion; and in this there'll be some sense. Now, still, the roving cats of Paris encircle him from the darkened aster gardens.

Pierrot's prowling among the gutted townhouses of the former nobility. (After Sicilian Vespers the stagnant calm.) One place in particular, only a few meters from the cemetery of the Madeleine, where the damask curtains are all shredded and the gold-tipped furniture is smashed and covered with cinders. There's a mantlepiece, it's been smeared with tar, but standing in front of the crazed mirror is an engraved invitation yellowed with years. He studies it:

You
are requested
to attend the funeral procession,
service,
and interment
of
Monseigneur Antoine-Paul-Jacques de Quelen,
head of the names and arms of the ancient
lords of the Castellany of Quelen, in Upper
Britanny,

juveigneur of the Counts of Porhoet,
nominee to the name and arms of Stuer de
Caulsade,
Duke de la Vauguyon,
peer of France,
Prince of Carency,
Count de Quelen, and du Boulay,
Marquis de Saint Megrin, de Callonges and
d'Archiac,
Viscount de Calvignac,
baron of the ancient and honorable baronies
of Tonneins, Gratteloup, Villeton, la Gruère and Picornet,
lord of Larnagol, and Talcoimur,
advocate, knight and vavasor of Sarlac,
high baron of Guyenne,
second baron of Quercy,
lieutenant-general of the King's armies,
knight of his orders,
menin to Monseigneur the late dauphin,
first gentleman of the bedchamber of
Monseigneur the dauphin,
grand master of his wardrobe,
formerly governor of his person, and of that
of Monseigneur the Count de Provence,
governor of the person of Monseigneur the
Count d'Artois,
first gentleman of his chamber,
grandmaster of his wardrobe, and
superintendent of his household,

which will take place, on Thursday the 6th of
February, 1772, at ten o'clock in the
morning, at the royal and parochial church of
Nôtre Dame de Versailles,
where his body will be interred.

De Profundis.

By this *objet d'art* Pierrot is not less than thoroughly
stupefied, since today is Monday, the 21st of January, 1793,
twenty-one years too late; and further, he doesn't think he's
ever heard of such a thing as a vavasor or a menin or a
juveigneur or, for that matter, of anybody with 35 titles
either active or in decline, and he didn't know who it was
that died, Monseigneur Antoine-Paul-Jacques de Quelen,
not personally, but certainly he sounds to have been more
important than the king himself. Curiosity of curiosities!
Ah, and speaking of Louis, now that it's 10:37 in the morning, he's just lost his head. Yes, down by the Jeu de Paume.
Soon enough they'll stuff him in quicklime just across the
street—how old exactly did they say he was?, thirty-eight
years four months and twenty-eight days—and someday
build a church. And more: some idiot—rumor does spread
like wildfire—has actually put the royal blood in his mouth
and pronounced it, yes, "shockingly bitter." What next?

Belles Excentriques

PLANTED IN PARIS when but an impressionable nine-teen, Maestro Mezzetinto has become quite gorged with the most romantic of phantasmagoria involving every sleazy byway in every pulsating arrondissement and all of the charming citizens who live there. His heart twitters, in particular, for the puckering young women of the 6ème, coquettes all, and in his most depressing little attic on the rue Saint-André-des-Arts he sets to painting as many of them as he can manage on canvases hardly bigger than pud-ding plates. The year is 1873. The boy has an irrepressible talent and his nightlong struggles are typically given their reward; although we must admit the girls' difficulty, posed for him with their garters agleam, in refraining from col-lapsing into laughter: because sporting an outfit designed with pink-and-chartreuse stripes that makes him hour af-ter hour quite perfectly resemble a peppermint stick the young man looks ridiculous. Ladies are all in agreement, however, that he's got very seductive stratagems. His aro-matic oils, for instance—collected in a little birdcage affair over the basin—intrigue them no end; when he douses him-self behind the ears with extract of tobacco their membranes infallibly begin to throb. It's true that he's deliciously tall, dark as an elephant's trunk in a rainstorm, possessed of a smile that instantly eradicates his sophistications. And the cheeks, ooh-la! Wishing urgently to rub his roundnesses (he's a smudge-pot from the Arabian Nights), desperate to count the soft hairs in the small of his back (he's an epigone of de Sade), the women contrive to alter their poses subtly during the long sessions in his parlor so as to produce a severe disturbance in his fuculation; and, indeed, soon the perspiration dripping from his wrists is smearing what he daubs and the salty drops flooding from his eyebrows are veiling over his sight. Poor Mezzetinto, how imperative is his need for a massage with pumice! But no chance—they torture him, continuing to display their rouged shoulders from a distance, permitting their lashes quite indecently to flutter whenever he looks up to gauge their curves, begging in twelve languages that he should supply them with mints. Mints and nuts. What a way to go through life! Two models in particular stiffen his paintbrush: Lady Flaminia, distant cousin of the ineffable Comtesse Chanterelle de Frangipane; and seemingly innocent, intoxicating, lizard-eyed Columbine.

Columbine, the one who has supplied him with books. In particular the printed scribblings of that infamous masturbator, Baudelaire, who, ten years ago, on the very day Mezzetinto first set foot in Paris, published an appreciation of M. Eugène Delacroix, as follows:

We know, don't we, that the era of the Michelangelos, the Raphaels, the Leonardo da Vincis, even the Joshua Reynoldses, is long gone, and the overall intellectual level of artists has dropped? Of course it would be unfair to look for poets, philosophers, and scholars among the artists of our day; but they could show a little more interest than they do in religion, poetry, and science.

Outside of their studios do they know anything? Do they like anything? Do they express anything at all?

Now, this very spirited stuff has gone right to Mezzetinto's principles—religion, poetry, science—so he spends half his time running around with *Les Fleurs du mal* in shreds at his armpit. And also pages that have just appeared in *Une Saison en enfer*. And also *Fêtes galantes*:

> L'implacable enfant,
> Preste et relevant
>   Ses jupes,
> La rose au chapeau,
> Conduit son troupeau
>   De dupes?

After which: in the turnip stalls of Les Halles he seeks for manifestations of The Almighty. Whereupon: as it delicately excresces from the peachy pores of Mademoiselle Columbine, in the afternoons, beneath his skylight, he studies, slowly, methodically, with the dedication of Lavoisier, of Pasteur, of Cuvier, until that poor woman is glistening, the

moistures of her passion of life. Itchy, finally, to change her
pose, she whispers one of their secret words...

But Columbine's figure has already graced many of the walls
of the Left Bank—on the rue Dauphine, the rue Séguier,
the rue Christine, the rue Bonaparte, the rue de Seine—
and also of the Right—on the Boulevard des Italiens, the
rue de Castiglione, the rue de Richelieu; because virtually
all of the Impressionists painted her. In particular Manet.
In his studios at 81, rue Guyot; and subsequently at 51,
rue de Saint-Pétersbourg; and thence down the block at No.
4, he immortalized her again and again: in *La Musique aux
Tuileries* (1862) she is positioned in a black-and-white
manteau and a cantonier with a red flower in its brim, next
to a seated gentleman with a moustache (Jacques Offenbach,
composer of *La Vie parisienne*) and behind a standing gentleman with a beard (the painter's brother, Eugène); in the
famous *Le Déjeuner sur l'herbe* (1863) was it not she who
posed as the semi-clad figure emerging from the water in
the background, that wise nymphet who has plagued the
searching intelligence of art historians ever since?; in a wa-
tercolor study for *Olympia* (1863) she reclined upon the
bed pouting, in the pose that would finally become Victorine
Meurent's; in *Le bal masqué à l'Opéra*, which he's accom-
plishing right now, she's going to appear at the extreme
left, her back flaunted to the viewer's eye, purely as a joke
in the role of Polichinelle (and the clown himself is posing

in drag as a blonde little kisser with striped stockings and a black mask!); and furthermore, the bulk of the 1864 still lifes were arranged upon Manet's rickety table by her gracious hand—peonies, grapes, eels, oysters, you name it. No, it's true everyone's had her, Manet, Sisley, Guillaumin, Boudin, Pissarro, old Corot twice on the Blvd. de la Rochéchouart—

> For the trailing, leisurely rapture of life
> Drifts dimly forward, easily hidden
> By bright leaves uttered aloud; and strife
> Of shapes by a hard wind ridden

—but little Maestro Mezzetinto is the one who's irrevocably in love. Her name, her visage, go rattling through his brain even when he's down on the corner of the rue Mazet picking out sugar beets and paying for having had his shirts starched. He's gone out of his mind for her and she, the blossom!, for him. But wait, chagrin d'amour, because if one afternoon in March he gives her a little book to hold in her fingers, *Sentimental Education*, while he's finishing what will be regarded as his masterpiece, *The Sortie of the Librarian* (see Blackmers, 1954 and Thurgood and Morivot, 1970), just as he's concluding his final strokes she takes liberty boldly to erupt, thus:

"Pooh, monsieur, infinite specimen of the pig! Do not you abuse me? Do not you stuff me with shame? I have brought myself only now from the rue de Saint-Pétersbourg—three hours that noble Edouard Manet makes me stand!—and has he not been très comique, indeed, yes, posing me as dear Polichinelle? But voilà, who is it that I have encountered outside in the street, right here by your filthy doorway, no sooner am I done, than the clown himself, heh? The clown, I tell you! Pooh, salaud! And what has he reported to me, that cornichon? What do you suppose he has reported to me in his simple-mindedness? He has told me that he has come immediately from you, is it not correct? That he has stepped directly from you, from this— pissoir! And what—pooh!? What does he tell me you are doing in this—pissoir, but painting someone else in my place, right here, upon this modelling stand, this very afternoon, some salami, some putain? And who are you painting in my place, monsieur, heh? Pooh! That harlot? Can it be that you are painting that harlot who makes my throat clamp up? Will I even degrade myself to utter her disgusting name, though she claims she is connected to a noble family? Pooh! I will not degrade myself. And can it be that, when you tell me you love only me, monsieur, salaud, slobbering your wild kisses all over my neck, it is the actual truth that you are thinking of her? Of that one, who smells like a sour fish, who has left her scent all over your rooms! Pooh, monsieur! How can it be possible, monsieur? That you can think of sluttish Flaminia when you whisper honeysongs to your devoted Columbine?"

The fact is, since everybody seems to think his life is a breeze, Mezzetinto's been having a great deal of trouble with the Lady Flaminia. Monday, Wednesday and Friday afternoons he's been sketching her, yes, certainly, because he knows Columbine goes off to Manet and what else is he to do, draw dumb oranges like that egghead Cézanne? Saturday evenings he takes himself flirtatiously to her apartment, so what, on the rue Boissy d'Anglas, just near enough to smell the ragôut from the kitchens of the Presidential Palace, after all one has to eat. "Pigeon," she simpers, "I would like, if you want the truth, to have a whiff of *your* ragôut!" (pouring out a couple of tinkling chalices of Möet et Chandon 1840) and white as a blancmange goes his face, he knows complications are on the way. He quickly pulls on his ecru chamois gloves, just in case. But she doesn't move a tendon, she's been lazing around since 6 o'clock with a pack of other lapsed ballerinas, all of them drowning in the ruffles of nostalgia, and they're lisping, "Blah blah blah jetée, blah blah blah pirouette, blah blah blah pas de chat," quite with an engrossment that's impossible for him to share. He's guzzling whatever anyone will pour with his heartbeat racing off, the name "Columbine" is inexplicably floating across the wallpaper in calligraphy that looks like snakes, awkward pressure is descending along the line of his colon and then curving inward to the point where his testicles kiss. Now suddenly Flaminia's getting rid of her guests, most suggestively fingering his shoulders, but he's imagining that the name "Columbine" is etched on the rims of the champagne glasses; and she's singing out to the crowd as they're waiting for the gilded cage of the elevator, "Oo-la-la-la-la-la *Giselle*, oo-la-la-la-la-la *Les Sylphides*." And he's finding it impossible to breathe. A bath, that's what he needs! Shampoo away that film of regrets. He tells her he wants a yummy-tub-tub and she coos like one of those cockatiels they keep on the Quai de la Mégisserie, running him out one with essence of lavender and a little ducky made of wood. Then, as he slides out of his clothes and feels his skin flush, she seats herself to do her croquignole. "Oo-la-la-la-la-la pâtisserie, oo-la-la-la-la-la bonbonerie, oo-la-la-la-la-la boulangerie, oo-la-la-la-la-la fromagerie!"—all the little rewards Terpsichore forbids us. He's splashing around in terrific positions, sighing as he crinkles a secret envelope of inward pleasure that's not yet been opened to reveal the black token of guilt. Is it, perhaps, that in truth he loves this one and not the other? Something about him goes limp inside when he prefigures to himself their weekly coital configurations—the soles of her feet pressed urgently against a wall; his face buried in her bookcase; his buttocks squarely upon the substance of her mammaries while her fingers are working behind his knees; her nibbling lips in his freshly-shaved armpits, and so on—and again the name "Columbine" appears in his imagination, this time swirling in a vortex beneath the surface of his bath with its tip in the hole where the waters will ooze out. "Mezzetinto, my darling," Flaminia has an introductory tone as she kneels at his tubside and punches his nipples with her fingertip, "There's something, there's a little secret, I've been wanting to tell you—" But now the very hexagonal tiles of the

116

bathroom are etched "Columbine, Columbine, Columbine" and he can't stop himself from breaking silence like a toaster's glass, "Do not speak, do not say a word. You mustn't love me, Flaminia, I cannot love you. Cannot. Will not. Not that I'm not full of respect for you, or that our liaisons haven't been too exquisite, but alors, I have pledged myself to another and alors, you will think I am lower than a worm and alors, it is she who must have me, down to the deepest marrow of my bones." Having delivered himself of this he gets out and pats himself dry: up, down, around, under. They go into the bedroom, join the curtains, latch the door. Unlatch the door, throw open the curtains. He paces. He stares eastward out the window as the winter sunset, banana yellow, is reflected in mauve panes across the street and the three-quarter moon, a meringue, lifts in the cloud-strewn sky. All of the denuded elm branches are tippling slightly in a wind, purple as sloes, when she whispers in cool tears, "But my darling, my innocent Mezzetinto: you have got me with child."

Imaginary thunderstorm. Brave sheets of crazed mirror hurled up, in which he can see his reflection a thousand times set against itself at obliquity. The sound, bouncing in his skull, of shrieking baboons, hundreds of the chattering blue-assed beasts, thousands, enough to fill the dimness of a jungle. Then his favorite Baudelaire:

Mais les vrais voyageurs sont ceux-là seuls qui partent
Pour partir; cœurs légers, semblables aux ballons,
De leur fatalité jamais ils ne s'écartent,
Et, sans savoir pourquoi, disent toujours: Allons!

But the real travelers are the ones who go
Only to be going; light-hearted as balloons;
They won't ever back away from the mortal show,
But, without knowing why, call forward: On our way!

At the Comtesse Frangipane's frowzy headquarters on the Quai Malaquais all seven parlormaids are aflutter. Tristitia has a long face while she waters the irises. Filesia is daydreaming of her boyfriend Ottavio and in consequence forgets to polish the brass candlesticks she's clasping. Bianchetta is stitching the hems of the drapery and twice thus far has poked the needle through the same finger. Rosetta has buried her head in a leatherbound *Salammbô*, but is finding it tedious—

"Moloch, tu me brûles!" et les baisers du soldat, plus dévorateurs que des flammes, la parcouraient; elle était comme enlevée dans un ouragan, prise dans la force du soleil.

Carparella is slicing ham upon a side table, and her tongue is adoring her lips. Vengolina is sliding a silk cloth up and

down the ivories of the piano, first having dipped it in vinegar. And in the vestibule, slender, modest, delicious little
Emilia with her blue bonnet upon her head neatly, sweetly,
welcomes plump distraught Lady Flaminia, four months
gone, heaving the lung audibly with every step, using one
hand to keep her furs off the carpet and another to pick
pieces of bonbon from the corners of her cheeks. And the
Lady Flaminia's going on about, oo-la-la-la-la-la, Maestro
Mezzetinto's thighs, but innocent Emilia hasn't got a clue
what a young man's thighs are for so she just repeats, over
and over, "I'm sure you'll be feeling better once evening
has come." What's that! A rattling signal from the landing!
As the Comtesse Frangipane threatens to make her appearance every other action stops: the chromatic fantasy of the
piano-cleaning is suddenly silenced, the glinty curtains
halted from wavering, the sweet thudding of the ham knife
arrested, the progress of *Salammbô* halted in page 314 without a moment's warning—

    Cette confusion de cadavres occupait, du haut en bas,
    la montagne tout entière

—and then in the quiescent intermezzo her long green
ancient skirts are heard to be rustling close upon the stairs,
slip, slip, slip—a fringe of her black ermine skims the surface of the eye—lengthy fingers belabored with fat ruby
rings—a bodice all tightened to severity—shoulders twitch-
ing—the chin sprouting hairs—an unirrigated grimace
upon the netherlip—The Comtesse approaching—The

Comtesse in place! "My too-tender cousine!—" her voice is as deep as a priest's, as adenoidal as the chant of an oboe, "Precious monkey, follow me into the drawing room, where I shall make haste to provide you with chocolate-covered ants!" The Lady gives a shudder but the old harridan, recounting the tales of her own eleven confinements, takes a seat upon an ottoman and insists, "My dear Flaminia, a dish of chocolate-covered ants every day until the delivery is the best galactagogue known to man." Whereupon a pink little box is brought in upon a silver tray, with a little dish and a tiny golden spoon, and the little dark things are built into a pile while Bianchetta, Filesia, Rosetta, Tristitia, Emilia, Vengolina and Carparella faint in an oblong at the Lady Flaminia's swollen feet.

And on the Right Bank: Monsieur Alphonse Granvilliers Scaramouche, the renowned civil litigator, is escorting his client, Mademoiselle Columbine, for tea at three o'clock in the afternoon on the fourteenth of the month to the Café de la Paix. The normally haughty waiters are obsequiously trying to pump fresh coins out of his lush pocket. Carriages clattering by are removing dignitaries—many of them, his friends, taking a moment to wave—from the Opéra up the road after the first act curtain of *La Forza del Destino*. Scaramouche twiddles his goatee. He casts his cold eyes left and right for prospective customers at other tables where steep croquembouches and butter-drenched écrevisses are being devoured. The young lady beside him is very confused, one moment turning her face away in shame and sighing, "Ohhh!" or "Hélas!" but the next blinking at him with all the innocence of a débutante's governess. "My very pretty demoiselle," says he, "Pray inform me what it is that I can do to bring assistance in your despondency." Whereupon she makes bold to say, mopping up a tear with a morsel of chiffon and commanding a waiter to bring her an orange upon a saucer, "I wish you, kind sir, to bring suit against a certain gentleman millionaire, the profligate Duc de Pierrot, whose vices, I may add, are so exorbitant he has quite lost the ability to keep track of them all. For years now, and altogether without knowing it, he has been supporting a young Umbrian artist who resides on the Left Bank, Mezzetinto by name. This Mezzetinto is a degenerate. It is my desire, for reasons I do not feel obliged to relate to you, to ruin him, to liquidate his arrogant prowess." She asks for a sharp little knife. "Old Pierrot lives in consummate luxury, he has no feeling for the street. His money flows to Mezzetinto through numerous filthy intermediaries, whose imbricate involvements are as close as the scales of a trout. The painter himself is pathetic, he has not a sou; if we take him to court, this is what we will get—" She shows her chalky palms. "But his patron is a man of bottomless reserves. Why should we not flatten the one by profiting ourselves modestly at the expense of the other?" She whizzes around the peel of the orange with the knife, removing it in a single piece which falls open on the white tablecloth before her. Then carefully she digests the fruitflesh. Scaramouche, observing his customer, is aghast at her talent. "My dear," proclaims he, displaying the orange peel significantly, "I believe you are ready to be married! But further, should I not be too delighted to help you, since I can plainly see your wounded heart heaving sadly within the sweet shelter of your breast."

Mezzetinto sits in his patron the Duc de Pierrot's dry garden, swatting away one bumblebee while he tries rapidly to sketch its mate. Baudelaire's been quoting Delacroix again, a serious painter must be able to draw a gentleman jumping out of a building faster than it takes that personnage to fall to the ground, and Mezzetinto knows it's only a matter of concentrating through the lens of his attention the spirit of the glance, the joy in sensing God's creation, the biological principle of thoracic vibration, and the poetic vision of the insect's delirious arabesque in a golden stagnant sunbeam. From behind, the bee he's been dodging swirls up silently, drops aster pollen secretly in his ear.

For quite some time the Duc de Pierrot has befuddled his admirers with a floppish lethargy and an expression of irresolvable tristesse. Pierrot, they think, *the sad one*. Nobody—with the exception of his trusted valet, Arlequin— knows the true cause of the dispensation: that four and a half years previously, near the town of M'Gouyah, upon a private exploration of the origin of the River Lefini (223 miles long), the duke having been bitten upon his right *Orbicularis oculi* by an insect of the genus Glossina, he is presently enjoying the experience of secondary Trypanosomiasis; having already (and bravely) endured the first and discomfitting stage of gross body swelling that was so easily disguised from his audiences by means of the loose-fitting gown they have all grown so happy to recognize. Now his vacant expression, a primary symptom, has become internationally familiar and beloved. (Pierrot, the sad one.) Most people are not privileged to witness the severe tremors of his *Masseter*, his *Orbicularis oris*, and his *Frontalis*, which occur on the average every six hours (Pierrot, the sad one); or, adulating his public mimes, to appreciate his lento enunciation or slugabed manners in the seclusion of his manuscript room. The special form of Sleeping Sickness the duke has contracted is called by the Congo natives, and many European travelers to West Africa as well, Nagana Disease (Pierrot, the sad one); it spreads like the Black Plague upon touch, almost always only to cattle; if only Arlequin were aware of its intense infectiousness he would scarcely sit up late nights massaging oils of fig-wort and fleur-de-lys into his master's *Gluteus maximi*. Nagana Disease, at any rate, is why we observe that once he has been hauled before Zozo the magistrate by vicious Monsieur Alphonse Granvilliers Scaramouche poor Pierrot practically snores through the hearing (Pierrot, the sad one), and why his valet gives the appearance of being as itchy as a hyena. Moreover, old Zozo hasn't been sitting behind the bench for forty-one years to take insults so, mortified by Pierrot's sloppy costume and Arlequin's gaudy one, he slaps both duke and valet with contempt citations, making a brief speech on the proper display of cuffs and buttons before the seals of the law. Attempting politely to protest, Pierrot collapses (Pierrot, the sad one) in a dreaming heap. Zozo tosses the case out. Arlequin considerably overpaying his master's fine with violent hiccoughs, Zozo is moved to retire to his chambers and pry open an old bottle of Vouvray 1812 he's been saving for a special occasion. The long and the short of it is, there being no waking defendants, Columbine can't presently get her satisfaction at the Fount of Justice; Pierrot snores blithely while he's pickpocketed on the way to his calèche; the lawyer gets roaring drunk with the judge and confides a marital secret; and Arlequin, stopping on his way homeward at the Charcuterie la Frigousse, eats so much macaroni it seems as though his pants will pop.

But one thing at a time—first the marital secret, soon enough the valet's abysmal digestion. Marital secret: The Lady Flaminia is not, as one would suppose, *une demoiselle violée*. According to documents on file at the Ministère de la Qualité de la Vie, she was formally connected to one Marcel Hilaire Bœufneuf, a seller of ladies' handbags, at 4:30 p.m. on May 11, 1870, in the town of Cabourg. Not at all a happy moment, she sees retrospectively. She has already been in the business of bearing him three children (What's this?, slavish domesticity!, so what would the ballerinas say if they knew what their friend had been doing after the matinées!), though with shoulders as slender as a fawn's the so-called husband is surely no more than a milquetoast. And is she not at her old tricks again—for Boeufneuf, with lazy tears trickling out of his decrepit eyes, as Baudelaire would put it, is adroit enough to have been the father of what she's dragging in her belly. Her affair with Mezzetinto has certainly been a *coup de passion* but behind her pleasurable madness there is motive: if she can procure him (with his great quivering thighs) as a legal husband the great litigator Monsieur Alphonse Granvilliers Scaramouche, on her behalf, can challenge the authenticity of the papers that insipid toady from Cabourg will wave. And if not, she is strapped for life to a creature who plucks his own eyebrows.

It happens at about this time that Columbine catches sight of Arlequin using as a public facility a sunny cranny in the Palais-Royal. She's really doing nothing but her business in that location, making way out of the apartment of the great litigator Monsieur Alphonse Granvilliers Scaramouche (where the chaises-longues are upholstered in cashmere), but it would be dishonest not to admit outright that the valet's pink presentiment, swollen well beyond normal proportions and promising the very greatest of aesthetic satisfactions, throws her sensibility quite out of the orbit of routine affairs. What a sculpture worthy of Versailles: he's contrived to have the spray arching over a peach tree—splendiferous!—and to be humming nothing other than her favorite ditty, "La donna è mobile."

But now to twist in the great intestinal tract of social alignment. The subtle game called "Beauty Makes Me Desperate," a moist geometry of feelingful proportions: (Everybody's in the gargantuan Louvre.) (1) Columbine's crying. She stands in front of Jean Auguste Dominique Ingres' *Baigneuse*; and she weeps enough tears to float away the City Hall because (1a) she has not been able, by pressure upon the Duc de Pierrot, to punish wicked lusting incontinent Mezzetinto; (1b) the Impressionists—Manet, Corot, Pissarro—having heard of her plotting against one of their band no longer wish to copy up her form; (1c) darling Mezzetinto himself is followed everywhere by that crapaude, Flaminia, whom he appears pathetically to adore; and (1d) the painting in front of her is a reminder that her best years are lost, lost and irretrievably lost. (2) The Lady Flaminia's crying. She totters in front of Leonardo da Vinci's *La Joconde* and exudes enough tears to float away the Louvre itself, principally because (2a) although it's true her yen's for Mezzetinto, alas, his is, too; also (2b) she gets more pregnant every minute; and (2c) she cannot conceive a method for unburdening herself of the vapid Marcel Hilaire Boeufneuf. (3) Maestro Mezzetinto's crying. He stands in front of Michelangelo Merisi da Caravaggio's *La Mort de la Vierge* and weeps enough tears to sink the Île de la Cité not because its beauty o'ersweeps his ambition but because he is trapped between two necessary impossibilities called women. (4) The Comtesse Chanterelle de Frangipane is crying. She stares at the *Winged Victory of Samothrace* (third century before Christ) weeping enough tears to fill a liqueur glass because (4a) someone has been steaming brussels sprouts in her kitchen all morning and (4b) even though she has despatched a footman all the way to Fortnum & Mason's, Piccadilly, she can't get lemon grass for dinner. (5) The Duc de Pierrot does not feel at all well at this point and wishes he could be crying ("It is often the case that the tear duct becomes clogged with excrescences from swollen sinuses in the anterior portion of the parieto-occipital fissure" [Hartzfeld and Nicolson, 1898, p. 1133]), but he sobs drily in front of the *Saint Sébastien* of Andrea Mantegna because of its intensity of stoniness. And (6) Arlequin is pouting and flailing and crying and wailing, beneath the *Venus de Milo*, because the macaroni has made him profoundly constipated, has it not?, and his tears are sufficient to submerge the city of Paris.

So he brings himself to the Champ de Mars, where the rusting sunset is filtered through blankets of chestnut trees. He wanders and backtracks and tiptoes over ferny ground until he comes to a glade where no witness can see. There squatting eagerly he lifts his rainbow garment over his shoulders in one swift movement and squeezes out a black long thrilling steamy coprolith for dada.

…On which spot exactly, on 28 January, 1887, the first dent of the pickaxe is made toward the erection of the Eiffel Tower. Among the first dignitaries escorted to the top, September 10, 1889, are Columbine and Arlequin, who have become fantastic lovers, the most famous couple since Louis XV and the Marquise de Pompadour. Eiffel himself is there, dining with Thomas Alva Edison at Brébant's. Gounod's at a table nearby. Glorious silence, spreading sunset all round, the quivering excitement of new vistas, new futures, unimaginable tomorrows. Gounod sits down at the piano, improvises on Musset:

> Assez dormir, ma belle
> Ta cavale isabelle…

and nobody leaves the dream until four o'clock in the morning (Charles Braibant, *Histoire de la Tour Eiffel*, Paris: Librairie Plon, 1964, p. 87). Sacré! They can spy all of Paris, that carnival of neighborhoods. They imagine to themselves they can spy all of uncertain, restless, optimistic Europe. The wind buffets the structure making the experience seem perilous, acute, unforgettable. Down in the tiny streets life is still an escapade: the Duc de Pierrot has been cured by stork egg omelettes prescribed by Docteur Pantalone, a wise old practitioner from Strasbourg; and he has married the Comtesse Chanterelle de Frangipane—a perfect duo, who cannot even imagine the idea of lacking for anything. Monsieur Alphonse Granvilliers Scaramouche has been promoted to the bench and has developed primary syphilis, but he's enjoying it. As for the Lady Flaminia and Maestro Mezzetinto (with his thighs still quivering in his pink-and-chartreuse striped suit) they're contentedly ensconced in the rue Laplace, at the Sorbonne's rump, on top of the restaurant *Ancien Paradis*—which serves the finest andouillette in all of France (though every afternoon it's true the ingrate goes searching for a better while his wife takes lectures in neuroanatomy from Charcot). In moments of reverie, not infrequent, the painter muses to himself how overwhelming life has been. And he rehearses something of Baudelaire's he can't get out of his mind:

> Pendant que le parfum des verts tamariniers,
> Qui circule dans l'air et m'enfle la narine,
> Se mêle dans mon âme au chant des mariniers.
>
> While the breath of green tamarinds
> Swelling my nostrils, filling the atmosphere,
> Mingles with the song of mariners in my heart.

In the iris garden the children, the twins Lelio and Lalia, play with papier-mâché puppets of all the family friends—Scaramouche, Pierrot, Columbine, Arlequin—gay puppets and also yellow marbles and stuffed horsies too, as they're dreaming with enthrallment of the beginning of the twentieth century.

Acknowledgments

I should have been at a loss in writing this book without the impressive work and generosity of Mr. James Trager and the assistance of Mel Gordon's replete *Lazzi: The Comic Routines of the Commedia dell'Arte* (New York: Performing Arts Journal Publications, 1983), from the lines of which I have made frequent happy, if irresponsible, departures. An earlier article, "The Adriani Lazzi of the Commedia dell'Arte" by Gordon with Herschel Garfein (*The Drama Review*, March 1978) was an inspiration. I am indebted as well to the staff of the Reading Room of the British Library, Great Russell Street, London; Ms. Meredith Chilton, Curator, the Gardiner Museum of Ceramic Art, Toronto; The Pierpont Morgan Library, City of New York; the William Robarts Library of the University of Toronto; and Mr Ian Richardson.

Philip Church has been a stalwart friend to me and to this book.

Of the numerous textual resources I have consulted, the most pertinent follow:

Charles Baudelaire, "Eugène Delacroix," trans. by Joseph M. Bernstein, *Antaeus*, No. 54, Spring 1985, and *Selected Poems*, Harmondsworth: Penguin, 1975.

Jean Anthelme Brillat-Savarin,*The Physiology of Taste or Meditations on Transcendental Gastronomy*, trans. M. F. K. Fisher, New York: Harcourt Brace Jovanovich, 1978.

Jeanne Louise Henriette Genest Campan, *Memoires sur le vie privée de Marie-Antoinette, suivis de souvenirs et anecdotes historiques sur les règnes de Louis XIV, de Louis XV et de Louis XVI*, Paris: Bibliothèque des memoires relatifs à l'histoire de France pendant le 18ème siècle. Also *Memoirs of the Court of Marie Antoinette, Queen of France. By Madame Campan, First Lady of the Bedchamber to the Queen.*

From the Third London Edition; with a Biographical Introduction from "The Heroic Women of the French Revolution," by M. de Lamartine, Member of the Executive Government of France. London: Henry Colburn. Philadelphia: A. Hart, late Carey & Hart, 1852.

Duc de Castries, *Le Testament de la Monarchie: l'Agonie de la Royauté*, Paris: Librairie Arthème Fayard, 1959.

Correspondance Secrète Inédite sur Louis XVI, Marie-Antoinette la Cour et la Ville de 1777 à 1792, Publiée d'Après les Manuscrits de la Bibliothèque Impériale de Saint-Pétersbourg avec une Préface, des Notes, et un Index Alphabétique par M. de Lescure, Tome Second, Paris: Henri Plon, Imprimeur-Éditeur, 1866.

H. Despaigne, *Le Code de la mode*, Paris: H. Despaigne, 1866.

Gustave Flaubert, *Salammbô*, Paris: Garnier-Flammarion, 1964.

Hieronymi Fracastorii (Girolamo Fracastoro), *Syphilis sive Morbus Gallicus*, Verona: 1530; translated as *Siphilis*, St. Louis: The Philmar Company, 1911.

Daniel Gerould, ed., *Gallant and Libertine: Eighteenth-Century French Divertissements and Parades*, New York: Performing Arts Journal Publications, 1983.

F. W. J. Hemmings, *Culture and Society in France 1848–1898: Dissidents and Philistines*, London: B. T. Batsford Ltd., 1971.

Nicholas Hilliard, *A Treatise Concerning The Arte of Limning together with A More Compendious Discourse Concerning Ye Art of Limning by Edward Norgate*, Wansbeck Square, Ashington, Northumberland: Mid Northumberland Arts Group in association with Carcanet New Press, 1981.

Gertrude Jekyll, *Garden Ornament*, Antique Collectors' Club, 1984.

Carl Köhler, *A History of Costume*, New York: Dover Publications, 1963.

Princess Lamballe, *Secret Memoirs of Princess Lamballe: Being Her Journals, Letters, and Conversations during her Confidential Relations with*

Marie Antoinette with Original and Authentic Anecdotes of the Royal Family and Other Distinguished Personages during the Revolution, edited and annotated by Catherine Hyde, Marquise de Gouvion Broglie Scolari in the Confidential Service of the Unfortunate Princess with a Special Introduction by Oliver H. G. Leigh, author of "French Literature of the xixth Century," etc., Washington & London: M. Walter Dunne, 1901.

D. H. Lawrence, *The Collected Poems of D. H. Lawrence, Vol. 1*, London: Martin Secker Ltd, 1928.

Ludovico Leporeo, *Leporeambi nominali alle dame ed accademie italiane*, Bracciano, 1641, quoted in Giovanni Pozzi, *Poesia Per Gioco: Prontuario di figure artificiose*, Bologna: Il Mulino, 1984.

Allardyce Nicoll, *Masks, Mimes and Miracles*, London: Harrap, 1931 and *The World of Harlequin*, Cambridge: Cambridge University Press, 1976.

Robert A. Paul, "The Eyes Outnumber the Nose Two to One," *The Psychoanalytic Review*, Vol. 64 No. 3, Fall 1977, 381–90.

Enzo Petraccone, ed., *La Commedia dell'arte: storia, tecnica, scenari*, Naples: Riccardo Ricciardi, 1927.

Donald Posner, *Antoine Watteau*, London: Weidenfeld & Nicolson, 1984.

Alex Preminger, *Princeton Encyclopedia of Poetry and Poetics*, Princeton: Princeton University Press, 1974.

Jane Roberts, *Drawings by Holbein from the Court of Henry VIII*, Johnson Reprint Corporation and Harcourt Brace Jovanovich, 1988.

Jean-Paul Sartre, *Baudelaire*, trans. by Martin Turnell, New York: New Directions, 1950.

Winifred Smith, *The Commedia dell'Arte*, New York: Benjamin Blom, 1964.

R. Spongano, *Nozioni ed esempi di metrica italiana*, Bologna, 1966, excerpted in Giovanna Angeli, *Il Mondo Rovesciato*, Rome: Bulzoni editore, 1977.

Andrew Stiller, *Handbook of Instrumentation*, Berkeley: University of California Press, 1985.

Robert F. Storey, *Pierrot: A Critical History of a Mask*, Princeton: Princeton University Press, 1978.

Arthur Symons, *The Symbolist Movement in Literature*, introd. Richard Ellmann, New York: E. P. Dutton and Co. Inc., © 1919.

Paul Verlaine, *Selected Poems*, trans. by C. F. MacIntyre, Berkeley: University of California Press, 1970.

Theodore Zeldin, *France: 1848–1945*, Oxford: The Clarendon Press, 1977.

MP

Toronto, April 1998

Murray Pomerance

Murray Pomerance was born in Hamilton, Ontario, and lives with his family in Toronto. He is the author of numerous books, including a bibliography of Ludwig Bemelmans and a collection of fourteen chapbooks called *The Complete Partitas*.

He is currently at work on a book on the films of Alfred Hitchcock.